The Widow's Tale

MICK JACKSON

KT-377-291

ff

faber and faber

First published in the UK in 2010
by Faber and Faber Ltd
Bloomsbury House
74–77 Great Russell Street
London WC1B 3DA
This paperback edition first published in 2011

Typeset by Faber and Faber
Printed in England by CPI Bookmarque, Croydon

A CIP record for this book
is available from the British Library

ISBN 978–0–571–25441–5

2 4 6 8 10 9 7 5 3 1

THE WIDOW'S TALE

When I ran out of the house I don't think I had any real idea where I was going. Although I must have had an inkling that I was doing more than just popping out, or I wouldn't have packed a bag.

By the time you get to my age you pick up your keys, purse, specs case, etc. quite instinctively whenever you set foot out of the front door. But I'd also managed to grab a couple of fistfuls of clothes and stuffed them into a hold-all, so I must've known that I didn't intend to be back for at least a day or two.

Great chunks of the journey are decidedly patchy. But I do remember winding down the window at one point and screaming. I was having trouble breathing. No – that's not quite right. I felt as if I was losing my mind. So I wound down the window and put my head out, in the hope that the wind in my face would help snap me out of whatever terrible and terrifying place I'd got myself caught up in. Then I remember screaming, long and hard, out into the night.

I'm just relieved I didn't cause an accident. Honest to God, I could have easily killed myself and anyone else who happened to cross my path. That stupid Jag is too bloody big and too bloody powerful. I've never liked it. But I'd left my lovely little Audi round at Ginny's, so the Jag was all there was.

Erratic.

That's the word I imagine the police would have used if they'd encountered me. 'The crazy woman in the stupid car was driving erratically when we pulled her over' is what they would've written in their report.

I remember finding myself on the M11 – a motorway for which I hold a fair bit of affection, if that's not a totally ludicrous thing to say, since I also have tremendous affection for other things, such as old brooches and small furry animals and even one or two people. But one way or another I found myself heading north on the M11. Then it was just a matter of whether I stopped off at Cambridge, or turned right and headed over towards Walberswick and Southwold or carried on up to the north Norfolk coast. And it was clear straight away which option I'd take.

Prior to that I'd just wanted to get the hell out of London. I'd somehow managed to find my way onto the M25, then headed east. I remember that series of soulless underpasses near Waltham Abbey. Then off onto the M11. Then up here.

I filled the tank somewhere just short of Cambridge and asked for directions. And perhaps because he was dealing with a woman – and, come to that, a woman with a puffy, tear-stained face – the young lad in the garage simply suggested I follow signs for Norwich, then pick up signs for any of the towns along the north coast. Then I left him to his magazine and the two of us carried on with our lives.

So by then I must have been a little more coherent.

Although I'd be hard pressed now to say with any confidence whether it was eight o'clock or midnight – only that it was probably somewhere in between.

If the rest of the journey is vague it's a different sort of vagueness, born out of exhaustion. Emotional exhaustion, perhaps, but quite different from the lunacy of that first hour or so. I remember reaching the coast road and turning west along it and, a little later, pulling off into the village and squeezing down the narrow lanes. And suddenly being aware of little houses all around me, with their lights out and, presumably, people sleeping in them. I remember pulling up by the quay, yanking on the handbrake and turning off the engine. And how incredibly quiet and dark it was. I didn't even get out to stretch my legs or fill my lungs. I just sat there and listened for a good five or ten minutes. Then I climbed into the back seat and pulled my coat over me and apart from turning over once or twice in the night the next thing I remember is waking up about six o'clock this morning, with the sky just beginning to lighten and me dying for a pee.

I've never been particularly big on breakfast. A cup of tea and a ciggie and I'm fairly happy, so this morning was a regular breakfast, just without the cup of tea. I'd snuck out onto the saltmarshes to relieve myself. Then sat in the car for a little while. I strolled up and down the quay a couple of times. And eventually headed up into the village.

I suppose by then I'd decided to see about some accommodation. My original plan was to book myself into the hotel, for nostalgia's sake – just for a night or two. But as I was wandering up and down I saw the little letting agents. And I thought, why the hell not? So I went back to the car and checked myself in the mirror, to see precisely how deranged I currently looked. Then, on the stroke of nine o'clock, as soon as the girl flipped over the 'Open/Closed' sign, I sauntered in.

She showed me round three quite different places – one huge, very swish and terribly minimal . . . one ramshackle affair on the edge of the marshes . . . and this rinky little place in the middle of the village, which was by far the cheapest but the price was really neither here nor there. The reason I plumped for it is the fact that it's tucked away. Which is rather strange, given that I only legged it out of London last night because I felt so dreadfully hemmed in. But clearly being tucked away up here in Norfolk is quite different from being hemmed in down there.

Back at the office – or shop, or whatever you'd call it – whilst the girl was tapping away at her keyboard I slowly leaned forward to have a peek at her screen. As far as I could tell, the cottage wasn't booked for a clear month or so. The girl did her best to stop me looking, as if she had personal access to the mainframe of the bloody Pentagon, but I'm long past giving a donkey's dick about what some girl her age thinks of the behaviour of a woman of mine.

I've taken it for a week. God only knows what I'll be up to seven days from now. I'm currently finding it difficult getting from one minute to the next. It was only when I'd shut the door behind me and dropped my bag on the floor that I finally felt as if I'd landed. Then promptly burst into tears. Which is possibly some kind of record of restraint, on my part. I've usually had at least a couple of crying jags by mid-morning.

The only thing on my to-do list right now is to get my head down and grab a little shut-eye. I don't want to hang about. Don't like waking from a nap to find it any darker than when I closed my eyes. I find that troubling in the extreme.

On the first page of the 'Welcome Pack' I'm reliably informed that this 'fisherman's cottage' was once home to a family of nine, which is clearly a veiled way of telling all those idiots who'd rented the place, imagining that it could quite comfortably accommodate two adults and two children, to quit their whining and abandon any hope of getting their money back.

But the cottage really is incredibly tiny. As I come down the stairs I have to lean back, into a sort of limbo, to avoid smacking my head, and I'm only five foot five. Anyway, a family of nine may very well have squeezed in here at some point, but that's not to say they were particularly happy as they sat at the fireside, mending their nets or whittling sticks or whatever they did to while away the hours. They were probably paupers and utterly miserable. There's enough room for me, but I wouldn't want to be inviting too many guests around for dinner. It's a widow's cottage is what it is. Maybe I'll carve a little sign out of the breadboard and nail it up above the front door.

The walls' many lumps and bumps are concealed beneath several acres of woodchip. The carpets are of the industrial variety. I have taken down one or two framed pictures to avoid offending my aesthetic sensibilities. They now languish in art-prison, beneath the stairs. They should count themselves lucky. At least they have some hope of parole for good behaviour, which is more than can be said for the half-dozen plastic air-fresheners which I found tucked away behind various curtains and perched on top of cupboards, all now bagged up in the outside bin.

The single bookshelf offers the usual bank-holiday reading – P. D. James . . . Jean Plaidy . . . Winston Graham. I can't say I've ever met anyone who's actually read a Winston Graham. I imagine they're published exclusively for men, to read on their holidays in England. Not to read, perhaps, but to hold in their lap while their wives read. Or until they fall asleep.

A little later now. I'm not entirely sure what time it is. I took my watch off earlier to do a bit of washing-up and forgot to put it back on. But it's getting dark.

There's a tiny TV, with quite a reasonable picture. But I'm resisting turning it on. I'm still a little stunned by the fact that I'm actually up here. And my new surroundings are giving me something to chew on. Otherwise I'd have to have the TV on. Or the radio. Or possibly both.

Christ but it's cold. I spent half an hour this morning wrestling with the controls, trying to generate any sort of heat, but the whole system is run on Economy 7, which is next to bloody useless. My attempt at running a bath was an utter failure. All I'll say is that if that boiler isn't capable of providing enough hot water for me to poach, chin-deep, at least once a day then the two of us are going to have a serious falling-out.

Lit a fire which brightened things up a little, but at this rate the small bag of coal and the two or three logs are going to be used up in no time at all. So I have started a little list: 'Logs . . . coal . . . kindling', closely followed by 'booze . . . fags'. Maybe those last two should go at the top. I added 'Milk . . . bread . . . etc.' almost as an afterthought. I'm not very big on eating at the moment. The drinking remains quite constant, but the eating comes and goes.

Called in at both pubs last night. The first has been heavily gastrophised and is nothing like how I remember it, with too many lights and too few people making altogether too much noise. I suspect the place is roundly despised by the locals as the clientele seems to consist almost exclusively of boaty types and second-home owners. Whoever they are, they certainly didn't lack self-confidence, on any number of issues. You must've been able to hear them halfway down the street. And they seemed to take quite a bit of interest in me. Not to the point of actually speaking to me, of course. Just sly little glances in my direction, as I sat in the corner, doing my crossword, steadfastly ignoring them.

The other pub – the Lord Nelson – is more traditional and doesn't seem to have changed too much, with a low ceiling and barrels of beer propped up behind the counter and lampshades that haven't been wiped in twenty years. The kind of place John would've liked. But at least the drinkers at the bar were fully engaged with one another and didn't seem to give a toss about me. Perhaps it was because I was onto my third or fourth drink by then, but as I sat there I could feel myself begin to relax a little. To the point that I started to look up from my paper and peer around the place. And when the barman came along and took my empty glass he gave me a smile that made me feel, perhaps quite mistakenly, that there was a real kindness to it – so much so that I very nearly burst into tears again.

It's true what they say about the kindness of strangers. In fact, to be honest, I haven't the first idea what it is they say about such things. All I know is that some unsolicited kind word from the chap behind the counter in the newsagent's or the boozer has a way of lifting the heart, and breaking it at the same time.

Of course, I'm an utter wreck at the moment, so my judgement is probably a little skewed. The emotional stuff I can more or less weather. At least you can convince

8

yourself that it's somehow helping you let off some steam. It's all the other stuff – the panic attacks and so forth – I can't be doing with. I find it hard to put a positive spin on that.

When I left London in such a hurry I was aware that I'd been seriously jumpy for a good couple of hours. I often am these days. I hate this time of year, when it starts to get dark before the afternoon's even over. I'm afraid of the dark. Can you credit it? I'm sixty-three and I'm frightened of the bloody dark.

But it was worse than that. I'd had a bath, with a few essential oils dribbled into it ('Yes, I'd like an oil to stop me being terrified all the time . . .'), and had a bit of something to eat. I was watching telly and I could feel myself getting more and more agitated. I don't think it had anything to do with what I was watching. I can't even remember now what was on. I just had this irresistible urge to get up and start moving about the place. Like some wild animal in a cage.

Then, suddenly, it seems I'd made a decision, and I was grabbing clothes and swearing and locking up the house. Then I was in the car, and heading north as quickly as possible, which was already too late. Because I needed to be out of London . . . *now*. Needed to be far, far away – immediately. With luck, I might just about manage to get clear of the city without actually killing somebody. And if not, then what the hell.

Whatever propelled me felt utterly instinctive. Almost primitive. Which makes it sound quite natural and even reassuring. But it wasn't. It wasn't like that at all.

I bought a bottle of Gordon's and a box of tonics from the Spar shop this afternoon, along with a couple of bottles of Sauv Blanc, a few nibbles, etc. The woman on the till was quite impassive but I have a funny feeling that round here one's alcoholic purchases are quite closely monitored. Ah well – fuck 'em. For all I care they can put a big blackboard up on the wall and keep a tally of my daily intake. I'll write it up myself.

I assumed I'd also be able to pick up a few bags of coal there, but for some reason they don't stock it, so I had to drive a couple of miles out to some windswept garage. How do you cope, I wondered, if you don't happen to own a car? What if I never quite muster the courage to leave this neck of the woods and end up hanging about until the old legs pack up? I'd have to have it delivered, I suppose. I'd be the old dear with her face up at the window, waiting for the coal.

I was halfway to the garage before I noticed something flapping on the windscreen. A parking ticket. And suddenly there I go again. That terrible tripping-up of oneself, when my first thought is that I'm going to get an earful from John for being so stupid. And the next thought is, Well, actually, no. Far from it. Because John is dead, and therefore not about to give a stuff about parking tickets or any other thing.

The whole sequence of thoughts is over in a flash. It's as if I'm just footling along, come round a bend and disappear into a walloping great hole. It's the same hole.

I just keep finding new ways of approaching it. If I have a hunch what's coming I can sometimes steer myself around it. Somehow give myself a fraction of a second in which to swerve. But most of the time I just go sailing in.

So yet another of the nation's unsuspecting garage employees is forced to witness the strange, snivelling lady. Thankfully, this one was good enough to help me load the coal and logs into the boot of the car. From the forecourt I could see the sea all laid out below me and was tempted to have a little drive down there, but ultimately decided against it. Couldn't quite commit. So I drove back to the village and pulled up as near as possible to the cottage (which is to say, not very close at all) and discovered that the bags of coal in particular weigh an absolute ton and it took me about twenty minutes to drag everything down the alley to my widow's cottage, by which time I was dripping with sweat.

Parked the car in the village car park where I've been assured I can leave it all week without getting a ticket, but managed to scrape one of the wings as I squeezed through the gateposts. Strange. I scrape the paintwork of the car and it doesn't bother me. But an hour or so earlier I get a parking ticket and it feels like the end of the world.

I don't really feel like walking, or frankly doing anything much at the moment. But I thought I should at least get outside for ten minutes before the last of the daylight goes.

I think that's why I first fell for this part of East Anglia.

You have the sense of so much sky above you. So much space. Which can be a bit overwhelming. One feels exposed, somehow – vulnerable. But the saltmarshes, which are actually a good deal greener than their name suggests, take the edge off the bleakness. They give it a kindness. And there's that word again.

Winter suits this landscape. Winter and autumn. Those are the only seasons I've been up here. I'm not sure I'd be inclined to visit it any other time of the year.

I only walked a couple of hundred yards but it was enough to get clear of all the houses and hear the wind in my ears. The tide was in, which is not to suggest that there were waves crashing about the place, only that all the little creeks were full. The saltmarshes are like a sponge. When the tide comes in the ground turns soggy. The tide goes out and the sponge dries out a bit.

I was just wandering around when the sun came out for a couple of moments. Nothing spectacular, but enough to feel the warmth on one's face. I thought of that poem by one of the First World War poets – Owen, I think – called 'Move him into the sun'. About some poor wretch who's half-dead, and how one of his comrades suggests they drag him into the sun, to try and revive him.

Well, I closed my eyes and lifted my face to the sun and waited – for it to revive me . . . to heal me . . . to help me out in any shape or form. I could actually feel it failing to penetrate. Feel it failing to do its stuff. I think I could have probably stood there all afternoon and it still wouldn't have done me any good.

Now at least I'm tucked up by the fire. I'm tempted to do a bit of reading. But I know the moment I start I'll just nod off. I'm doing my best not to watch any telly. I'm not sure why exactly. It's not as if I consider the TV to be particularly evil or anything. It's just that if I watch it I forget where I am, and when I suddenly remember I go into a bit of a panic. Whereas if I just sit and stare at the fire I know that I'm here. I still worry, but after a while it's not so bad. Which must sound mightily pathetic, I'm sure, but right now that'll just have to do.

I walked over to Cley this morning, along the raised bank that swings out towards the water, then round to the east and south in one long crescent. The whole thing can't be more than a couple of miles in total, but for some reason it felt like quite an achievement, and required a fair bit of self-goading before I'd actually set out.

The walk itself was fairly unremarkable, except for the fact that I couldn't stop yawning. Perhaps it was some response to the cold, fresh air. Yawning, as I understand it, is linked to one's oxygen intake. But it quickly became quite ridiculous; like some peculiar compulsion. And something over which I had absolutely no control. After about the sixth bout I began to worry – that I'd end up in some hospital for compulsive yawners . . . or the subject of some TV documentary. 'The Woman Who Can't Stop Yawning' or something along those lines. Even now, as I bring it to mind, I can feel another one creeping up on me.

I was pretty much the only person out there, bar some old chap with an equally ancient dog trotting along behind him – some unidentifiable mix, which I stopped and chucked under the chin for a minute. The poor bugger looked all in, and just determined to get back home and conk out in front of the fire. After I'd said goodbye and carried on I felt myself to be slightly lacking, as if I too should have a dog with me. A woman walking on her own looks a little . . . singular. Whereas if you're swinging a lead and you have some mutt bounding back and forth and sniffing hither and thither, one seems to make more sense, visually.

If I'd left London in less of a hurry I might have arranged to borrow a dog off a friend. Assuming, of course, they'd've trusted me with it, which is by no means certain. There should be places where you can go and rent a dog – just for the weekend. I'm sure the dogs would be quite happy with the arrangement, as long as you could reassure them that there'd be plenty of walkies.

There was a beautiful black lab out by the quay yesterday afternoon being dragged around by some dreadful woman. Titus, it was called. No one within half a mile could have been in any doubt about that. Can you think of a more pretentious thing to call a dog? I was half inclined to offer to buy the poor creature off her. She didn't seem especially enamoured of it. Then I considered just following her around until she tied it up outside a shop and nabbing it. I'm sure I could have made him happy and if caught, I'd anticipate a degree of leniency once the whole Titus thing was explained. I would've given him a proper name, like Barney or Bernie. Though I will admit that the idea of picking up a dog's poo and carrying it around, like a dog's own official poo-carrying servant, does make me want to retch. But it might just be worth it – for the company. And the unconditional love.

Anyway, I finally limped into Cley, no longer yawning but feeling a lot more tired than I probably ought to. And was sorely tempted to head straight for the boozer and have a little pick-me-up. Why not, for heavens' sake? I'm on my holidays. Unfortunately, I've currently got a strict no-drinking-at-lunchtime policy. In fact, I do my level best to put off the day's first drink until after 6 p.m., which some days, let me tell you, is near-impossible.

Christ knows how I'd've got through the last three months without alcohol. I probably wouldn't. I've got various pills in case of emergency – all properly prescribed and entirely above board. I keep them with me, or pretty close at hand, but I'd rather not if I can help it. I fully appreciate how I'm using booze to 'self-medicate', as a friend rather charmingly described it. But at least it's a drug with which I'm familiar. I know how it works and how to administer the appropriate dosage. And hopefully when to stop. But I can't pretend that there aren't some days when I start looking forward to that little sock to the head before I've even finished my breakfast, and think about it another couple of dozen times before six o'clock finally rolls around.

I stopped outside the smokehouse and peered in at all the smoked mackerel, smoked eel, etc. And all the pâtés and stuff they do these days. John was a big fan of smoked fish. Not that his was a particularly sophisticated palate. He would've eaten an old boot if it'd been smoked for long enough – and had a dollop of mustard or horseradish next to it.

I stood there, gawping through the window until I realised that someone in the shop was watching me. So I scuttled off over the road to the deli and had a wander among all those very expensive vegetables in their little wicker baskets and the jars of exotic pickles and hand-crafted biscuits, etc. They had a pretty impressive cheese counter, including a great hunk of Roquefort, to which I'm particularly partial. But I couldn't be doing with all the ordering and the chit-chat with the woman in her linen apron. I just knew that she'd be of the opinion that running a deli should involve a great deal of chatting. So I kept my head down and crept out of there.

For a while I just stood on the pavement. Having decided that I wasn't going to patronise either the smokehouse or the expensive deli and having barred myself from the boozer, I had very few options left, apart from turning round and doing the Widow's Walk back across the levee, when a little bus came bobbing down the lane.

I wouldn't have known that the bus actually stopped in the village if some old dear hadn't been standing a few yards ahead of me with her hand out, so the bus pulled up right next to us. The old girl jumped on and for a moment the bus driver and I just stared at each other.

'You getting on?' he said.

And the next thing I know I'm parking myself among all the old grannies as the bus hauls itself up the hill.

It felt quite odd. I can't remember the last time I took a bus anywhere. This one was called a Hopper – something between a minibus and a full-size affair. It looked rather boxy, with a too-high roof which, to the people we passed, I'm sure made us look like a bunch of loonies or some old dears on a day trip out from a retirement home (which perhaps isn't that wide of the mark).

I looked around at the other passengers. An oldish woman on the other side of the aisle smiled back at me.

'I don't usually go on buses,' I wanted to tell her. 'I'm not . . . you know . . . *poor* or anything.'

Actually, there's probably a decent PhD paper to be written about bus travel. Perhaps not so much in Britain, but certainly in the United States. Out there, particularly in the cities, taking the bus is a sure sign of impoverishment. Then there's at least thirty thousand words to be written about how the bus featured in the Civil Rights Movement in the late fifties – Montgomery and Rosa Parks and all that. And all the associations that 'Getting on the bus' had, and possibly still has, for political rallies and demonstrations. Not to mention the whole romance of sweeping across the country on a Greyhound. I don't imagine there's an equivalent here. Britain's not quite big enough to lose yourself in. Although, God knows, I'm doing my best.

But I have to say that as we rolled along I felt . . . in fact, I'm not at all sure what I felt exactly. Only that it wasn't unpleasant. I certainly didn't feel quite as conspicuous or solitary as I have done lately.

'Ye gods,' I felt like saying, 'I've only been here five minutes and I'm practically a local.'

This evening I took the scissors and cut off the lead to the TV. If it's there I'll always be tempted to turn it on, just as a distraction. This way, that temptation has been removed.

It was a symbolic little act, executed in the heat of the moment. But I checked – twice – to make sure it wasn't actually plugged in before making the snip.

The young slip of a policewoman who turned up on my doorstep three months ago would, I think, have preferred to have imparted the news indoors. In fact, I know she would because she suggested several times that we step inside, but I refused and insisted she tell me there and then what she was doing knocking on my door at that time of the morning.

Perhaps corralling people into their houses prior to delivering bad news was something she'd been taught at Police College out at Hendon or wherever they go these days. You can see their reasoning. You don't want people running up and down the road, screaming, first thing in the morning if you can possibly help it. But I stood my ground and raised my voice to such a pitch that she must have weighed up the options and deduced that, at this rate, forcing me back into the house was likely to cause more commotion than the very commotion she'd been trained to avoid. So she let me have it, as they say. Right between the eyes.

Several times, over the last few months, in those little breaks I occasionally take from feeling sorry for myself, I've thought of that young policewoman and what a dreadful responsibility that must have been – for a girl her age to have to tell a woman thirty-odd years her senior that her husband is not coming home.

A couple of things will always stay with me. Firstly, after she'd finally got round to telling me what had happened, just how strangely the world around me proceeded to behave. The very air seemed to bend and buckle. The walls of the house . . . the trees out in the garden . . . the car parked on the drive were all of them gripped in this same tremendous convulsion, as if their physical being was suddenly called into question – or their molecular structure undermined.

The other thing I remember is a terrible urge to barge past the policewoman. I remember looking over her shoulder and up into the sky. Did I imagine that's where John was? In the lower ether, somewhere between this world and the next? And that if I hurried, and somehow managed to jump high enough, I might yet catch him – and stop him from abandoning me?

I've no idea. I don't imagine I had much more idea then. Whatever drew me away from the house seemed to have very little to do with me. What stopped me was the policewoman, who, to give her credit, was pretty bloody strong. Perhaps that's something else they teach you at Police College – how to position your feet to withstand the not inconsiderable force of the newly bereaved.

As she held me I noticed, for the first time, a male colleague standing a few yards behind her. So it turns out that even if I'd managed to bundle past this young woman I would've been rugby-tackled within another yard or two. And all my moaning and wailing would've been confined to the actual garden, beneath fourteen stone of policeman, among the buckled air and the unreliable trees.

That first convulsion was followed by others – almost like after-shocks – which came around every five minutes or so. One part of the brain seemed to grasp what had happened straight off the bat. But some deeper part of me clearly failed to take it in. As the hours passed the shocks' frequency slowly diminished, but their force was stubbornly maintained.

The whole emotional turmoil was soon stifled by the arrival of friends and family, whose very presence seemed to dampen things down. Then you become preoccupied with the need to get in touch with those people who aren't yet aware of the situation. And distracted with the necessary tea-making for all these people who've suddenly filled your home.

The next four or five days were all focused on the funeral. And, not surprisingly, the day itself is the next big spike in the emotional graph. What I'm about to say will, I'm sure, sound quite idiotic. Well, there you go. If nothing else, it might serve as a reminder of how, in such times, the sensible and the completely bloody ridiculous have a tendency to coexist.

I'm not sure how consciously I ever thought it, but there's no doubt that I took some solace from the fact that John would be there, at the funeral. In a way, I imagined we'd be reunited. Isn't that just about the craziest thing you've ever heard? And of course, he *was* there. Almost within touching distance. With nothing but a half-inch of timber separating us. But we certainly weren't about to be reunited. And when, at the end of the service, they took up that coffin – the one I'd personally picked out of the brochure – and the music started up again, and they began to carry him out of the church, even before we'd gone anywhere near the chapel of rest, with all its automated rollers and mechanised curtains, the actual removal of this man from my life struck me like a ton of bricks. And I heard myself shouting. And, again, found myself being held . . . being restrained. And that's when I knew that this really was the end. And that he was never coming back to me.

Yet, an hour or two later, there you are at the reception, keeping an eye on the catering (the *catering*, for Christ's sake!). And a day or two later, you're having meetings with accountants and solicitors. Doing Death's administration. It goes without saying, of course, that all these days are punctuated with spontaneous fits of tears – some private, some not so private – but everyone around you conspires to keep you busy. Which at some point is going to have to involve sorting out the house . . . or, specifically, sorting through his belongings. So, at first, I just filled a few black bags with his clothes (most of which I'd never particularly liked anyway) and bundled them off to the charity shop, and dragged a few more bags up into the attic to be sorted out later, so that they were out of sight. Then, again unconsciously, I simply set my sights on getting through to the end of the year. On getting through Christmas. Because, as people never tire of telling you, Christmas will be the time you miss him most.

So, having shrieked and screamed in the very first instance, and having been endlessly hugged and patted by what felt like the world and his wife, then helped up the aisle to see him off, and having crawled through the year's darkest days to the right side of the winter solstice (when I could at least tell myself that the days were getting longer and that there was sunshine and warmth somewhere up ahead), I found myself standing in a New Year. And it suddenly dawned on me that that was not the end of it.

I had somehow allowed myself to imagine that my reward for enduring the hell of those first few weeks of bereavement would be some sort of relief, or even reprieve. That John would be returned to me and I could tell him just how miserable his absence had made me. And we would just sort of muddle through from there. But sometime in the first few days of January it suddenly came home to me that there was to be no reward, no reprieve. There would just be as many years of bereavement as I could stand, stretching off into the future, in my new, husbandless life.

I was lying in bed this morning, drifting about in that rather uncomfortable zone between sleeping and waking, when I remembered a few bits of food I'd left out in the kitchen the night I bolted. And the milk, etc. in the fridge that would soon be going off. Luckily, the lovely Lynn will be calling in this afternoon to do her bit of cleaning, so when I finally dragged myself out of bed and dressed I rang and left her a message, warning her of the sort of scene which was likely to confront her, so that she didn't panic and call the police.

Since pitching up here I must've received a good dozen or more texts and messages, expressing varying degrees of concern. As luck would have it, the village is a genuine blackspot, re mobile reception, and the only place you're sure to get a signal is the grassy mound just back from the quay. So I have the perfect excuse not to actually speak to anybody. The phone has rung only twice, when I've inadvertently strayed into civilisation's range, way out on the marshes. But on both occasions I've just let it ring until the answering service clicks in.

I've sent texts or left messages for any people that matter, explaining that I've decided to get out of town for a few days and that I'm completely hunky-dory, which is therefore only half a lie. There are no doting sons/daughters/brothers/sisters. And, frankly, most of my friends and acquaintances are a bloody shower – an opinion which I am using as an excuse for not giving much more than a damn about hurting their feelings. I can't for the life of me think how I managed to gather about me such a bunch of second-rate and hopeless individuals. The only one that I truly care about – the only one guaranteed not to look back at me as if I'm speaking bloody German, no matter what I have to say – is Ginny. And right now even she's no use to me.

Just after breakfast, for the first time since I got up here I dared to peek in my diary, just to check that I hadn't missed some important appointment. One or two things might require a little shifting and shunting. But, to be honest, there's nothing earth-shatteringly important. In fact, I'm beginning to appreciate that my running away up here will create very few waves at all.

It's death's intransigence that's so hard to swallow. That's the brick wall you keep coming up against. The death arrives, all done and dusted. And, frankly, how you deal with it is neither here nor there. There's no negotiation. No higher court to whom you can appeal.

About two o'clock this afternoon I had a little stroll out on the saltmarshes, which is fast becoming my daily constitutional. Just half an hour or so's wandering about under that big grey sky, with nothing between me and the horizon except the odd long-abandoned fishing boat.

Most of the modern boats are penned in together by the side of the creek, just a couple of hundred yards from the village. Evidently, January is not the prime month for sailing, so they don't seem to be doing much right now, except keeping their heads down and weathering the winter, a bit like me. You have to walk a fair old way to leave behind the mad rattle of the lines on their masts. Some days I can almost convince myself that it's a sound of which I'm fond. I try and tell myself how very evocative and atmospheric it is. Other times, I'm not so sure, and you can be seemingly miles away and the wind will suddenly pick up, and that mad rattle will be upon you and it can send a chill right down your spine.

I was mooning about out there just now when I remembered going for a walk with my mother and father when I was little – no more than six or seven years old, I'd say – on the moors somewhere, most likely up in Yorkshire where my father's family originally came from. I remember running off and finding some little hollow – a shallow little trench, but quite natural and lined with grass.

I remember lying down in it, and being able to hear the wind roaring above me, but my being perfectly sheltered from it. I'm sure I couldn't have lain there very long. Just long enough to appreciate how wonderfully out of the way I was, as if I had found a little fold in the landscape. But I felt I could happily lie there until the end of time.

Woke up last night about four o'clock, feeling profoundly rotten. Sometimes, if I have a sip of water, or a pee, and get my head back down pretty sharpish I'll slip back off to sleep. But if I allow myself to start thinking as I did last night then I'm basically screwed.

To be fair, half the reason I woke up in the first place was the amount of white wine I'd ingested a few hours earlier. My whole body felt as if it'd had a good, long marinade. It was quite clear that there was no earthly chance of me nodding off again. But I gamely lay there, in the dark, fretting and panicking, for what felt like hours.

An old woman went by the window just now, pushing a bicycle which was laden with bags of shopping. She looked like a refugee. There was no way in the world that she'd ever be able to pedal that bicycle, even without the two hundredweight of shopping. It was essentially a sort of zimmer frame with wheels. Anyway, she kept on putting one foot in front of the other and on the whole seemed quite pleased with her progress.

This morning I just about managed to convince myself I had the necessary stamina to venture out beyond the village, if only for an hour or two. I'd read somewhere about a church a couple of miles down the road with what are said to be sixteenth-century graffiti of ships. So I climbed into the Jag and headed out past Cley, along that lonely stretch of road where the creeks come right up to the tarmac on one side, and on the other there's nothing but the occasional little row of houses looking out towards the sea.

Someone once observed how I'm drawn to places that are half in and half out of the water. At the time, of course, I thought she was completely crackers, but as I drove along this morning that innocent little remark came back to me and, not for the first time, I felt a twinge of guilt which suggests that she might have had a point.

The actual church is a solid-looking piece of architecture, not particularly pretty – or particularly modest, considering the location. But I suppose north Norfolk was a fair bit busier and more God-fearing when they built it. I parked the car on a patch of grass right beside it and marched up the steep little path.

The actual 'graffiti' is on the back of pews which have all been arranged for viewing quite close to the main door

– essentially just a series of scratches etched into an earthy wash of ochre, which makes the whole thing feel quite primitive, as if there might be the odd drop or two of ox blood mixed in with it. The ships themselves are pretty rudimentary – skeletal and quite fragile, with a little rigging and rectangular flags. Before actually setting eyes on them I'd somehow assumed that they'd been done by grown men as they struggled to stay awake through some interminable sermon – predecessors of Alfred Wallis, drawn in the naïve style. But, of course, why on earth would someone who spent his working life out on a boat return home and scratch ships into the furniture? The moment you see them it's fairly evident that it was the handiwork of children, or more specifically, young boys. The galleons they aspired to one day climbing aboard.

There aren't that many of them – maybe four or five ships in total. The sort of vessel a stick figure would sail. But I found myself inordinately moved by them. Perhaps it was the thought of a child's crewless ship drifting through the murky ochre for four hundred years or more.

Certainly, they're far more touching than any number of stained-glass windows or spires or communion tables. In a way it's a shame that they've been dragged out of their original position. I would have quite liked to have got down on my hands and knees and peered round a corner to view them where they'd been secretly scraped into being.

The old rood screen is also on display, in various sections. Eight pairs of saints, or possibly apostles, standing around, doing that beatific thing with their hands. What's shocking is that all their faces have been scratched out, presumably in the Reformation. Strange, considering the mutilation is only done to an image, but one can't help but imagine the physical sensation of the knife on one's actual face.

I dropped a few coins into the wall as a donation, then smoked a cigarette out in the graveyard. And on the way home I made a bit of a detour and called in at Holt, principally in search of a better bottle of wine than those on offer in the village shop. Wandered into a second-hand bookshop to have a quick nose about. I hadn't gone in there with any particular objective, but perhaps because of my little visit to the church in Salthouse, I found myself loitering around the Art section, and within a couple of minutes had found a rather lovely collection of Holbein prints.

I was still leafing through the book when some old chap approached the counter. The couple who run the shop were sharing the duties – about my age, perhaps a tad younger. And they'd just about finished totting up the bill for the bloke's books and putting them in a bag, when the old chap spotted some etching on the wall behind the counter. It was some wide open landscape, which could've been any old place (I had a quick glance at it myself a little while later as I left the shop) – the South African veldt as easily as the Fens. But the old fellow seemed quite taken with it and became highly animated. And asked the shop owners where it was.

Without missing a beat they both said, 'Where would you like it to be?' in unison. Which struck me as wit of the highest order.

Needless to say, the old duffer didn't think it half as clever as the rest of us. And once he'd got his change he gathered up his books and limped off in a bit of a grump. But his lack of humour didn't appear to diminish the shop-owners' spirits, and they went back to their newspaper and their pricing, or whatever it was they were up to. And I carried on leafing through my Holbein.

I honestly don't know why I didn't just buy it. It's some weird superstition, whereby I have to return it to the shelf and leave it a couple of days, and in the meantime gauge how much I want it. And if I decide I really do want it and I go back and it's still there then it was meant to be.

Anyway, I started to think to myself how this couple – let's call them David and Jennifer – given the right circumstances, could quite easily become friends of mine. Judging by the quality of books on their shelves they're pretty sophisticated. And, as has already been noted, in possession of a biting wit which is a prerequisite for anyone I'm going to respect enough to call a friend. And I began to imagine me and David and Jenny laughing and drinking in some rural boozer. Me and David and Jenny having dinner at my widow's cottage and talking deep into the night.

I even imagined myself working in the bookshop a couple of days a week – just, you know, to get me out and about. And my being party to the bookshop banter – arguing, in a light-hearted manner, about whose turn it was to make the tea or coffee, or pop out to buy the biscuits ('...and this time get some *proper* bloody biscuits – the sort that have chocolate on the top').

Perhaps that's another reason I didn't buy my Holbein. I wanted the excuse of going back. They had one of those portable gas stoves that make such a racket when you light them. I could think of a lot worse places to spend my Tuesday mornings than a cosy little shop like that, with decent people, surrounded by books.

But I wasn't halfway home before I started having my doubts – and began to pour cold water on my little fantasy. What if Dave and Jenny didn't want an odd number at their dinner party? What if I didn't quite fit in – numerically or otherwise – with their mah-jong evenings? Wasn't sufficiently bohemian for the Jazz Night out at Cromer? Or sufficiently scruffy for the Folk Club at King's Lynn?

I'd parked up, locked the car and turned around before I realised that something was the matter. That the line of trees before me had a gap in them. More significantly, that when I looked to my left the original gap had been miraculously replanted, only for a new gap to appear along the way.

It always takes me a moment or two to work out what's happening – that these tiny omissions are the mad little outriders bringing news of even greater ocular failings and visual fireworks. I was in my mid-twenties before I understood that it was some sort of migraine. Giving things their proper name can sometimes make them less threatening. All the same, I now simply know what's coming – that very soon it will feel like I'm looking out at the world through a frosted window, or have been staring at the sun.

It's that initial moment of realisation that's always the most alarming. If I can get to a tap pretty quickly and splash cold water onto my face and over my neck and shoulders I can occasionally nip it in the bud. To be honest, I'm not convinced it makes the slightest difference, but it's something to cling onto. The alternative is just to surrender and let it ride roughshod over me.

Whatever – the whole thing is deeply distressing because . . . well, because blindness, even temporary, partial blindness, is bound to shake you up. And today, when I finally worked out what was happening I suddenly felt incredibly insecure and alone up here, without anyone near me that I could call on, just to hold my hand.

I know that every previous episode has passed and that my sight has always been fully restored, but that doesn't stop me worrying that this one might prove to be unshakeable. By the time I was back at the cottage, half my vision was gone. I almost clattered into a couple of people on the high street and only succeeded in getting the key into the lock on the front door by looking off to one side in order to line it up in my periphery.

I should probably just be thankful that I don't have those real head-banging, debilitating three-day migraines that some people suffer. For them the flashing lights are just the beginning. Like the flashing lights at a level crossing. The barriers come down and they know that it's going to be one very long and uncomfortable wait. With me, it's usually over within forty-five minutes. In the meantime I can keep my eyes open and watch as the blind spots slowly evolve from fizzing little chains into great blocks of oblivion – and gradually recede from the centre of my vision. But it's a show I've seen too many times already. So I tend to put a damp cloth on my neck and lie down in a darkened bedroom and listen to the radio, or try to doze for a while.

Now, here I am an hour or two after the event, and my thoughts are still a little jumbled. If I'm in company I often experience some difficulty arranging a sentence, as if caught up in a mildly dyslexic fog. A bit like being hungover, but rather disconcertingly, without having had a drop to drink.

This morning, as I desperately splashed cold water over my face up in the bathroom, in a futile bid to head it off, I caught a glimpse of myself in the mirror. What I saw was not unlike those vandalised saints I'd seen earlier on at Salthouse, with their faces completely obliterated and all their features gone.

Those first couple of years we used to have the most incredible arguments. Proper plate-smashing, snarling, spitting, cat-and-dog sessions. Like Liz Taylor and Richard Burton in *Who's Afraid of Virginia Woolf?*. For some reason Friday nights used to be our preferred evening for a bit of a dust-up. We'd spend an hour or two loading ourselves up with booze, then off we'd bloody well go.

Of course, I can't for the life of me now remember what it was that so exercised us. Quite possibly just the uncontainable rage of two people suddenly confronted with the fact that this was it. This spouse, with their infuriating little habits and boundless ignorance. God, no! we must've been thinking. Not fifty years of this. Let me out!!

After two or three years our scraps died down a little. I'd like to say that we learned how to properly appreciate one another, but it's just as likely we simply resigned ourselves to our miserable lot. We would still have the odd set-to now and again, just to keep our hand in, but we tended not to go in for so much of the histrionics – the whole yanking-down of curtains/upending of tables/etc. Why bother, when a couple of choice words or a well-timed grunt could do just as much damage? And by then we weren't necessarily trying to provoke another round of screaming and shouting. All we wanted was to gently rake over the coals of deep despair.

If, five years into a marriage, you still don't know how to get under the skin of your spouse – how to plug straight into one's loved one's battery of insecurities – then you really haven't been paying attention. Similarly, when you're on the receiving end, you learn soon enough how to tell real rage from rage's impersonation. Real tears from the am-dram equivalent.

By the time we celebrated our tenth anniversary we barely fought at all. And I have to say I rather missed it. I missed caring that much, either way.

Speaking of Richard Burton, they had some idiot on the radio the other day being supremely dismissive about him. I can't remember who he was. Some thrusting young critic, I imagine. But it rather struck me how it's apparently quite acceptable these days to be perfectly pissy about Burton's films and performances, which rather depressed me. I mean, did you have to be around at the time to appreciate the man's talent? If you watch those films now, out of context, are they completely meaningless?

There's no doubting that when you see a film with Burton in it you know pretty much what you're going to get. But that's why people bought their tickets. He had that ticking internal mechanism which meant you couldn't take your eyes off him. James Mason was the same. You never hear people singing the praises of him either these days. And it makes me feel dreadfully old to be sticking up for actors who, not that long ago, were generally considered to be gods.

I have a cassette of Burton reading *Under Milk Wood* at home somewhere. I should've brought it with me. I never was that big a fan of Thomas's poetry – all that maudlin, sub-Yeatsian babble rather gets on my nerves. But I do like some of his prose. And *Under Milk Wood* definitely works, in its own weird way. Thomas and Caitlin were another pair of proper scrappers. I once read someone's account of visiting them out in the sticks. And how at dinner, after a couple of drinks, Thomas started picking on Caitlin, and she started having a go back, until finally the two of them dragged each other off to the kitchen and proceeded to knock seven bells out of one another. Caitlin finally emerged, triumphant, and limped back over to the table, pinning her hair in place, and said to their guest, 'Well, thanks very much for coming to the aid of a lady.' A minute or two later Thomas reappears, with a split lip and a black eye, and carries on where he'd left off. No doubt telling everyone what a genius he was.

Today, it seems, is laundry day. The resident washing machine is practically Edwardian and whilst I've put most of my clothes through it, I don't feel it's to be trusted with one or two items. So I've been doing a little washing by hand.

There's an extendable wire rack in the bathroom which pulls out from the wall. But the moment I touched it the bloody thing flung itself off into the bath. I carefully replaced it, but it's clearly incapable of bearing the weight of a single sock. It was an hour later before it occurred to me that every visitor to this place has probably had exactly the same experience, but no one has had the balls to point it out to the agents for fear of losing their deposit.

I'm half inclined to take it out the back and set fire to it. The little bugger has left me with a blood blister right under my thumbnail, where it nipped me. And all the clothes are strewn over the backs of chairs and radiators. I feel like I'm a character in some kitchen-sink drama. I should be wearing a headscarf and moaning, in a Northern accent, about my having a bun in the oven and him blowing all the housekeeping on beer.

The other thrilling new development is that I've become a newspaper-buyer. I forgot to pick one up the day before yesterday and it meant I had to sit in the pub and read a book, rather than do my precious crossword, which irritated me no end. At home we've always had them delivered and to be honest I've just never quite got round to cancelling them.

One of the articles I read today concerned some report into rocketing dentists' charges. And how, as a consequence, more people are simply not bothering to go at all. It failed to mention how a fair proportion of the population aren't particularly keen on going to the dentist in the first place and ready to latch onto any excuse which comes their way. The same report claimed that due to the hike in dentists' prices we're increasingly inclined to indulge in a bit of DIY dentistry, citing one character from somewhere like Leicester who's extracted a dozen or more of his own teeth with a pair of pliers.

Now I think most people would agree that check-ups, at the very least, should be free to everyone, especially those who are short of cash. But it's equally clear that the fellow to whom they referred is a certifiable nutcase. And that if he hadn't been pulling out his teeth with a pair of pliers he'd've only got up to some other form of self-mutilation, like lopping off his toes with a pair of secateurs.

Anyway, the obsessive buying and/or reading of newspapers has always struck me as a peculiarly male trait. Along with hushing one's wife in mid-conversation to listen to the news on the radio, as if this was all dreadfully important and the newsreader was addressing them personally.

I'm not entirely sure where it comes from – this rather inflated sense of self-importance regarding current affairs. It's perfectly admirable, I'm sure, to try and keep abreast of what's going on, both nationally and internationally. But at the very heart of it there is, I think, a delusion of mammoth proportions, which is that by keeping up with the news one is in control of it, and therefore in control of the whole wide world.

Perhaps it goes back to all that Evelyn Waugh/P. G. Wodehouse gentlemen's clubs stuff. Perhaps, when men sit in their favourite armchair on a Sunday morning and plough through some impenetrable piece about what's cooking in the Ukraine or Tanzania, they imagine themselves akin to some cabinet minister.

Whatever it is, it's clearly in their chromosomes. When the health department of the local council has to break into some semi-derelict house because of the terrible smell and the fear of conflagration, is it ever a woman they find lost among the towers of rotting newspapers? No. Generally speaking, it is not.

I once went on a retreat, when I was in my mid-twenties, to a convent somewhere out in the Welsh borders. Considering that this must have been during the late sixties and all the other sorts of retreats that would have been open to me, electing to hang out with a bunch of nuns seems like a terribly conservative choice. But given that most of the alternatives would probably have involved me sitting in a circle with dozens of other people, talking about their feelings and, no doubt, some beardy guru doing his best to try to get into your pants, I can still see why I made the decision I did.

I was never particularly religious, and there was never any danger of me signing up for full nun-dom (not that they would have wanted a young woman as soiled or worldly as me, I'm sure). But I was certainly curious – about a life reduced to such simplicity . . . mainly solitary, predominantly silent, and almost entirely spent in devotion to something outside of oneself. I can't be the only person ever to wonder if there isn't some solace to be had in such a life.

Anyway, I recall turning up and a certain disappointment that instead of being given a cell with a bare floor on which to sleep I was shown into a fair-sized room, with a large desk and a sink in the corner and a single bed, complete with mattress and sheets and everything.

I don't believe it was an order with a strict vow of silence, but personal contact was so minimal and there was so little to say on the few occasions I did encounter anyone else that I'm sure I mustn't have uttered more than a handful of words the whole time I was there.

When you've finished your breakfast and you're back in your room by six-thirty there can suddenly seem to be a great many hours in the day. But I would just sit at my desk and slowly pick away at my poems or short stories that I was still convinced would one day make my name.

Once or twice a day I'd go for a walk around the grounds, and stand and stare meaningfully off towards the Black Mountains or sit on a bench and breathe in the scented air. And after lunch I would curl up on my narrow bed and have a little nap for half an hour. I don't recall ever going into the village, even though it was no more than a couple of miles away. Perhaps I felt that being among such philistines might have threatened to corrupt my newfound purity.

There were various services throughout the day and I remember one of the sisters inviting me to take part in them. I declined. I would have felt such a fraud. But I did go along to the chapel on one or two occasions and sat at the back, just to hear the singing. I remember how much that moved me. As I'm sure it would have moved any mortal who didn't have a heart of stone.

I'm not entirely sure what the nuns got up to the rest of the day. Mainly praying, I imagine. With perhaps a bit of gardening or cooking thrown in, just to break things up. The other presiding memory of my visit is of someone locking the main door at nine o'clock in the evening, which made me rather anxious. I've always been slightly claustrophobic. But I found that by leaning out of my window and following the maze of drainpipes down to the ground I could reassure myself that, if absolutely necessary, I could shimmy down to safety, and this helped calm me down. Then I would lie in my bed, with my hands held stiffly at my sides, to keep them out of trouble. And with every passing day I could feel myself become a little more immaculate.

Each morning at about five-thirty I'd be woken by a light tapping at my door. And one of the sisters would pop her head into the room and I'd hear her whisper, 'Are you with us, dear?'

It was an odd thing to hear first thing, before you were properly awake. But each time I'd hear myself whispering, 'Yes,' back into the darkness. 'Yes, I am.'

Then the door would close and I'd be left wondering what exactly I'd consented to. And if, by some chance, I really had managed to consign myself to a life of prayer and the occasional bit of gardening, whether that might not be such a bad thing after all.

I mention all the above because only an hour or two ago I noticed how I'd set out the table, with the paper and pens I bought in Holt all neatly arranged, and it occurred to me that one way or another, and what with the cutting of the TV cable, I have recreated that same desk where I wrote my poetry when I went on retreat the best part of forty years ago.

This place is so God-damned *cold*. You'd think a house so small, with walls so thick, might actually keep the heat in. But it's as if all the misery endured by the fisherman and his fisher-wife and all their fishy children has somehow impregnated the walls. And my little widow's fire isn't about to make much of a dent in it.

But I am undaunted and first thing every morning now I clear away the previous day's ash, just like a trillion put-upon women back through history. And, as often as not, I usually manage to find a few red embers, and arrange a few bits of kindling around them. And before you know it, hey presto, we're in business again.

There are, I'm sure, worse ways to come around in the morning than by staring into the flames of a fire as it begins to take hold. As I sit and stare I do my best not to think about what I'm going to do with the day ahead of me. I try and put that off till lunchtime. By then I've only got the afternoon to worry about. The evenings are beginning to take care of themselves – namely, a trip to the pub, then back home for a bit of eating, more drinking and another hour or two of staring into the fire.

I'm a worrier. In fifty different ways I worry. About how fucked-up I am. About how fucked-up my future's looking. About all the extra pain that's waiting for me there. I have created for myself my own little . . . what am I saying, *little*? . . . my own *monumental* vortex of sickness and anxiety. And who on earth would deny me that?

My worries come in a whole host of shapes and sizes. There are days – an alarming number of days, let me tell you – when I feel like a stranger on earth. I have problems with reality (my number one problem with reality being that it is all too terrifyingly real). I feel raw. I feel alienated. Sometimes just getting from one moment to the next is an effort. And speaking of time. I think its gears are slipping. I'm not sure it knows which way is up.

Other than that, I'm doing just fine.

A friend of mine, who has had her own little difficulties over the years, passed onto me some little nugget of wisdom she'd picked up somewhere, quite possibly from a professional, which put great emphasis on acknowledging those occasional moments each day when you're not actually one hundred per cent depressed or desperate. When you take a sip of coffee, for example, or take a breath of cold, fresh air. Or you find yourself laughing, albeit involuntarily, at something on the radio.

The theory is, I suppose, that you begin to accept that such moments exist. Then perhaps start to knit these teeny pockets of hope together and focus on the good stuff, if only to give yourself some respite from all the crap. And slowly convince yourself that one's life is not, in fact, a wall-to-wall horror show.

Well, like I say, it's a theory.

I have enough objectivity, at least, to see that some of my little episodes are self-inflicted – in that I start niggling away at something until I find that I can't stop. I wind myself up into a sort of neurotic frenzy and make myself quite nauseous. Whereas other attacks just seem to land on me, like a meteorite. It's as if I smell something in the air – or briefly experience a strange metallic taste at the back of my throat – and before I know it . . . WHAM . . . I'm struck down in my tracks.

I have begun to use the phrase 'panic attack' in certain instances. I do now know that whilst it might feel as if I'm falling, I am not actually falling. And that even if I were actually falling, I will not, in fact, fall forevermore. I've had all of this pointed out to me. But, contrary to popular opinion, the successful identification of such a thing does not necessarily nullify it. Does not make it go up in a puff of smoke. So, I can be wheeling my trolley down the aisle of the supermarket and, without knowing why, feel the fear begin to creep up on me. And suddenly I'm off, slipping and sliding down my own terrible helter-skelter, until I think I'm going to pass out, and fall head first into the nearest freezer, among the pizzas. To be found, months later, by some despondent shelf-stacker, like one of those frozen corpses they chip out of glaciers. And what will the archaeologists make of me, I wonder? Will all their carbon-dating equipment and fancy micrometers successfully tell them what my story was?

Oddly enough, one fragment of my myriad anxieties is bumping into people. I'm not half as panicky up here.

Maybe it's because there are fewer people. Or maybe I'm just afraid of those people who might actually know me – who'll gravely enquire how I'm doing, whilst examining me to see precisely how screwed-up I am today.

Ah well. I'll just have to hide away out here in the sticks the rest of my life. And buy an old black bike to push my shopping back from the Spar.

One thing I really do worry about is that without John around to rein me in I'll slowly grow into some eccentric individual. Not eccentric, as in quaint and charming. Eccentric, as in just plain weird. Our marriage was far from perfect, but one way or another we used to contain each other's excesses. And now that he's gone I worry that I'll become wild and odd. Like that horrible fig tree we had in our back garden – the one which was so thoroughly strange and alien that I had to get someone to chop it down.

Losing one's husband really is a complete bummer. But let's look on the bright side. I've actually lost a little weight. Oh, there's loss of all sorts going on around here. Mind you, I wasn't particularly chunky to begin with. And unfortunately, after a certain age, when you lose a few pounds you don't look any younger. Just pinched and scrawny. And those mad, staring eyes don't help.

Sometimes I'd just be grateful if I could sit still for five minutes at a time without wanting to jump out of the window. I've seen a counsellor once or twice and, at Ginny's insistence, a whole host of hippie healer-types. I've been acupunctured, cranially manipulated, have had my feet and earlobes squeezed. And when, five minutes into whatever session I'm having, I begin to sigh or quietly sob I can detect a definite aura of smugness in my practitioner. They're thinking, Well, it didn't take me long to crack *this* one. All I'll say is, they overestimate their achievement. These days it doesn't take much to get me going – a lost cat/dog poster, sellotaped to a lamppost . . . daytime telly . . . about four bars of Rachmaninov . . . pretty much anything.

It's not that my healers' vanity particularly offends me. At worst, I've paid someone forty quid to rub my feet or knead my shoulders. If they want to imagine that, along the way, they've tweaked my crystals or realigned my chakras, well let 'em. I can think of a lot of worse ways of spending my cash.

Ten years ago – maybe more – I went along to a couple of evening classes in which we received solemn instruction in the art of sitting and breathing, etc. There was the odd minute or two in the midst of all that Omming when, if nothing else, the steady resonance in my skull was so sonically pleasing and all-pervading that any coherent thoughts were simply shaken off the shelf.

I've had another crack at it lately just as a way of trying to calm myself down. But, pleasant though it is, I have the feeling that I contain within me such vast reservoirs of pain and anguish that I could Omm non-stop from now till Christmas and I still wouldn't have drained off more than a tiny fraction of the stuff.

Probably the only point in my life when I've actually sat still for any length of time and felt quite happy, and perhaps come closest to a meditative state, was a year or two in my early twenties when I did a bit of life modelling for a friend of a friend. Simply writing that down seems, frankly, ridiculous. Like recording that I once did a stint as a secret agent or trained to be an astronaut. Life modelling now seems impossibly bohemian. The truth is I was terribly strait-laced – a rather serious young woman. And my entire family would have felt obliged to commit hara-kiri if they'd thought I'd been paid to do so much as remove a sandal. Which was perhaps the point.

A girlfriend of mine had been posing for this particular

painter but had to give it up as she was leaving town and asked if I fancied taking over. I went in to meet her – the painter, whose name was Annie – just for a cup of tea in the first instance, to see how we got along, and presumably for her to give me a quick once-over. But I remember my first proper session and climbing those narrow wooden stairs up to her studio above a shop and her leading me over to a screen for me to change.

I'd taken a dressing gown, as instructed. I undressed and put it on. Then I crept out and we chatted for another couple of minutes. Then Annie said something like, 'Right. Shall we get on?'

She showed me where she wanted me to stand and turned and went over to her canvas. And I understood that these few moments, while she busied herself with her paints and brushes, were there for me to disrobe. I was quite petrified. But I also remember feeling . . . well, rather excited. Not sexually, necessarily. Just a little thrill, in doing something so utterly unlike everything else in my humdrum life.

For the first couple of sessions I must have been terribly self-conscious, and found it hard just to sit still for half an hour at a time. But you begin to know quite instinctively when a particular pose is going to be unsustainable and Annie was perfectly accommodating. And once you're settled you get into the habit of just drifting off into your own little world. It might take five or ten minutes, but sooner or later I'd start thinking about books I'd read or planned to read, or little ideas of my own. I used to religiously carry a little notebook around with me, so that I could jot things down in it, and the moment Annie suggested we take a break I'd scoot over to my clothes and pick out my notebook and try and get down all the things I'd been desperately trying to keep in my head. Just little thoughts and observations, which seemed so important at the time.

But now it's the stillness I remember. That incredible stillness and my being comfortable in it. And as the afternoon wore on, feeling the rest of the world outside that room slowly fall away.

Even now, the merest whiff of turpentine takes me right back there. I remember the splattered paint, two inches thick, on the bare floor below the wall where she worked. The paint on the door handles, the electric kettle – everywhere. And I think what I wouldn't give to be back there, forty years younger, with my life spread out before me, when I could happily sit for hours at a time and all I really cared about was the next line of some half-formed poem. And what it was I had to say.

One of the surprises, re the sudden onset of widowhood, is finding that one no longer has to consult one's husband on every last decision. Whether to move house, how much soy sauce to put in the dressing, and everything in between. A couple of months ago I had a bit of a late night over at Ginny's. We'd been drinking and talking and before we knew it, it was half past one. Ginny suggested I stay over and I was about to object on the grounds that any disruption or act of spontaneity would, as always, be met with prolonged husband-sulking, when I realised that the whole sulk thing no longer applied.

With John gone, life is now an endless succession of options, none of which has to be presented to the household committee before being acted upon. This sudden sense of liberty, it almost goes without saying, can be quite bewildering. One feels like some creature emerging, blinking, from the deep, dark cave of compromise into the blinding sunlight of . . . well, what exactly? The blinding sunlight of *choice*, the cross-party mantra of modern politics.

But if one welcomes all these new options, one must also come to terms with the fact that one can no longer define oneself and one's opinion simply by placing them in opposition to whatever opinion one's husband happens to hold. You say the crime figures are up? Well, let's go and live in Sweden. (Q. What's that sound? A. The sound of no one listening/caring.) Well, dammit, if I'm not going to get a reaction, what the hell's the point in me being provocative?

My future, it seems, is frighteningly open to interpretation. On a bad day it is a bleak and empty desert stretching towards the distant horizon. On a good day it's the same desert, but with a couple of cacti to break things up a bit. Recently, a friend suggested I might get involved in the 'voluntary services', as if I were some old neddy that should be put out to pasture, as opposed to being mercifully shot. Perhaps she thought I might have a future standing behind the counter of a local charity shop – you know, as a way of *getting out of the house* and actually *meeting people*. With the greatest respect, I would rather chew off my own arm. Being surrounded by all that crochet and bric-a-brac. Not to mention the rest of the planet's waifs and strays.

Apropos of nothing, there's a woman in a certain charity bookshop in north London who is prone to barking. She has what my mother used to refer to as a bit of a habit. The first time I heard it I was picking through the History section. I spun around. Her colleagues were all carrying on as if nothing had happened. But I quickly worked out which one was at it. It wasn't difficult. She had another little bark as she headed up the stairs.

She seems perfectly fine, except for the barking. Quite a well-to-do woman in her late sixties, I'd say. I've been back two or three times when she's been on duty. The first bark, you suddenly remember. Then you sort of get used to it.

But now I feel guilty for having mocked her. And the good little angel on my left shoulder observes that whilst she might be prone to the occasional woof, on the inside she's probably the epitome of mental equilibrium. Whereas I rarely bark at all. But on the inside it's non-stop barking. In fact, I'm fairly howling at the moon.

It was only this morning that it occurred to me that, being up here where no one knows me from Adam, I could be just as adventurous with my past as my future. I could conjure up for myself a whole new identity.

I am, in fact, a famous photographer. Or a famous writer. But then people will only ask if they're likely to have come across any of my work. Unfortunately, I shall explain, most of my stuff's incredibly highbrow. Poems mainly. And all published abroad. I translate them myself. Except for the haikus, which I write in Japanese.

Of course, I needn't necessarily be famous. I could just be . . . interesting.

Actually, speaking of voluntary work, I quite fancy having a go at rebuilding some of those drystone walls. I must have seen someone at it on the telly, and was particularly impressed by the way they trimmed each piece of stone into the appropriate shape. The same way I once saw a bricklayer split a brick in half with a single clip from his trowel. I'd like to be able to do that. I'd like that very much. When I met a stranger and they asked what I did, I'd like to be able to say, I'm a bricklayer. A layer of bricks.

Last night, as I entered the Lord Nelson I noticed how the barman had already picked a glass out and was reaching up towards the gin's optic before I'd even opened my mouth.

Actually, I said.

He stopped.

I cast my eyes up and down the counter. These beers, I said. Are any of them female-friendly?

He drew an inch or so from one pump into a shot glass and offered it to me. It was actually quite tasty. Not half as bitter as one might think.

I supposed aloud that women tended not to drink pints.

He said that I was mistaken. And that these days many a young lady enjoyed a pint. Especially the lagers. Besides, he reassured me, a couple of pints now and again is very nice. Adding how good it is, every once in a while, to feel properly filled-up.

I held his gaze with steely determination. I must not, I told myself, glance down at this man's midriff. I have sneaked a peek before and since. Suffice to say that it comes as no surprise that this is a man who advocates the pleasures of being filled right up. This fellow looks like he's been filled up with a hose.

So I sat at my usual table, with my crossword and a pint of Woodforde's Wherry before me. And when I lifted it I used both hands to make sure I did not spill a drop. It's rather lovely. And not too fizzy. I doubt that I could drink two or three pints every night. I couldn't be doing with all that going to the bathroom. But it makes an interesting alternative to the old G & T. And my head wasn't at all fuggy this morning.

Perhaps I might develop a taste for it. Perhaps in six months or so I'll have the beginnings of my own lady's beergut. Nothing particularly imposing. Just a bump big enough to rest my pint glass on. As I hold forth on my day's bricklaying. And complain about the price of sand and cement.

A couple of months ago I did a bit of cursory Googling and tripped over some startling statistic, regarding how many women lose their husbands each day of the year. I've forgotten the actual number, but it was many more than one might have imagined. I have this picture in my head of a hundred newly minted widows popping up across the country the very same day I burst onto the scene. And every last one of us with that same stunned expression on our face.

Sadly, the fact that I'm not alone in losing my husband is of no comfort to me. I have no desire to get all sisterly about it. I feel not the slightest need to hold hands with all the other widows and make one great big daisy chain of grief. Suffering, I'm inclined to think, is a solitary business. And, I could be wrong, but I suspect that a fair proportion of the other widows feel the same.

I can't help but notice the continuing proliferation of roadside floral tributes. Either they're actually on the increase or I just tend to notice them more these last few months. I passed one earlier this week, just down the road from here. Some sorry-looking, garage-bought bouquet, still in its cellophane wrapper, slowly turning to dust.

Do the people who lay these flowers imagine they're

performing some public service? That their sad little posies are going to prick people's conscience and improve road safety? Or are they just hoping to provoke in all the passing motorists a few brief moments of empathetic sadness? Either way, they're deluded. Perhaps, suspecting that no one else actually gives much of a monkey's about their 'loss', they have gone out of their way to draw attention to it. As if, by spelling out their loved one's name in petals, they could make the world sit up and take notice, and that this might somehow siphon off some of the pain.

The first floral tribute I remember seeing was out near Barnes, a good thirty years ago now. A few flowers tied to a tree on the common. I hadn't a clue what they were doing there until some friend explained that the previous year some pop star had been killed in a car crash at that particular spot. It was just some teeny-boppers laying flowers at the site of the death of their idol. I'm sure they were very upset, and that they thought they loved him. But I mean really.

I imagine it's the same misguided instinct that was at work after the death of Princess Diana. When half of central London seemed to be carpeted with flowers. I can't be alone in thinking that that public outpouring of emotion was quite obscene in its magnitude. At the time, no doubt, there was much talk of some shared sense of sadness, but I thought then and still think that whilst there might have been the veneer of unanimity, beneath it simmered something almost sinisterly self-involved.

But at what point did the whole flower-laying concept shift from being something one did for famous people to something one did for one's own brother or daughter or son? I must have missed it. Although, if people are laying wreaths for complete bloody strangers it's only reasonable that genuine mourners be allowed to create a shrine for their own flesh and blood.

But now everyone's bloody well at it. A teenage boy is shot dead in some faceless city and before the police have finished cordoning off the area there's a gaggle of girls hugging one another and clutching single roses and grieving for the cameras. The body's barely cold and they're already mumbling their cretinous testimonials, about Darren's love of life and Darren's generous spirit. I think to myself, I bet you were never this kind to Darren when he was breathing. I bet you made Darren's life a living hell.

Call me old-fashioned, but, personally, I think floral tributes should be confined to the graveyard. Or the homes of the mourners. I think the front-room curtains should be drawn, according to custom, to signify loss, but also a desire for privacy. This is *my* grief. And my pain is *not* your pain. Go and get some pain of your own.

Everyone seems to want in on the emotional action. All I can say is, Give it time. Before you know it you'll have more grief than you know what to do with. And not the self-conscious, superficial variety for some TV princess you never got within a mile of. Or the boy from the year below. But the sort that takes a hold of you and inhabits you, like a sickness. That possesses a body so comprehensively that you'll feel yourself obliterated. And so profoundly, utterly peculiar, that you'll want to keep it to yourself.

I've decided to sell the house in France. These last couple of years we hardly used it. And when we did, we'd just follow the same deadly routine – a drink here, a walk there, etc. We knew a few people in the nearest village. But neither of us really liked them. And taking friends down with us was too much responsibility. That sounds dreadfully mean, I know, but the mind-numbing effort of being Mine Host for a full week just made me miserable. And late at night, after a glass or two too many we'd just end up having the same petty disagreements we'd had a dozen times before, guests or no guests.

Five or six years ago, when there was still work to be done on the place, that fact would give us a little motivation. Some shared purpose. And we'd talk about how, once it was all finally completed, we'd be able to sit back and appreciate it, but it was quite the opposite. We just realised how bloody boring it was down there. And when I lifted the toilet seat last year and found a rat skittering about in the bowl, that just about did it. I screamed and slammed the seat back down. Let's be honest, if you can't scream when you find a rat in your lav, when exactly are you meant to scream? John came huffing and puffing up the stairs, assessed the situation, then disappeared. And came back up the stairs a couple of minutes later, carrying his tool box.

What exactly, I asked, was he planning to do to the rat? Dismantle it? I don't think he knew himself. Anyway, not surprisingly, after that little incident I could never fully relax whilst visiting the bathroom. And the house's days were probably numbered.

To be honest, I'm half tempted to sell the house in London. It was too big when it was just the two of us. Although God knows where I'd go. A part of me thinks I should buy some little pad in Clerkenwell. Or on the river. Then at least I could walk to the cinema or the theatre or a restaurant. If you're living in a city, the argument goes, then actually live right in the heart of it. But then I'm sure I'd have young people pissing on my doorstep, or puking, or fornicating. Or whatever it is young people do these days.

The fact is I freaked out and had to leap into my car in NW3, so how the hell would I cope living even deeper in the city? Perhaps I could have a speedboat tied up on the river, with its engine gently ticking over. If I felt a bit queasy I could just jump into it and head for Kent.

I have no aching desire to raise chickens and grow my own potatoes, wherever one goes to do that sort of thing. And, apparently, I have my doubts about living in London. Looks like I'll just have to stay here in my bijou cottage until I decide where on earth I might feel comfortable.

Actually, I don't know why I'm talking about the theatre as if it's some major foundation of my cultural existence.

And that without it I'd, you know, simply go to bits. Twenty years ago I used to trot into town pretty regularly, to the West End and the South Bank. But I think half the time I was just fooling myself.

You do indeed have to kiss a lot of frogs. These days I find I just don't have the stamina. I had a little epiphany maybe four or five years ago, when I was penned in in the middle of an auditorium as some endless bloody Russian play creaked and groaned along. The maid was meant to be completely ditsy, which for some reason I found rather offensive – or just plain lazy – and each time she jiggled her boobs about or one of the other characters made some dreadful pun, everyone around me launched into this ridiculous guffawing, as if they'd just heard the funniest joke ever. I was thinking, This isn't remotely funny, you idiots. Why the hell are you laughing? And the only answer I've ever really come up with is that they'd paid good money for their tickets and they just wanted to show the rest of the audience that they were at least intelligent enough to get the joke. Or perhaps they just thought that over-the-top guffawing at dreadful puns is what you do in such a place.

Anyway, I found myself sitting there thinking of all the other, more rewarding ways I could be spending my time, like lying in bed or watching telly or doing the washing-up. And when the interval finally hove around I got to my feet and left the theatre and never really looked back.

Life's too short to pretend to enjoy something when it's clearly pigswill. At least at the pictures if the film's complete twaddle you can walk out without feeling like you've wasted more than a couple of quid.

These days it's so rare for something to genuinely surprise me at the theatre. Without it being deliberately, self-consciously shocking. And frankly when you've seen one troupe of naked, shaven-headed eastern Europeans rolling round the stage in some controversial new production of *Hamlet* you've kind of seen them all.

I'm getting old. I've seen too much. I'm unshockable. Well, perhaps the first of those three statements is true. I used to be quite pally with this woman who was a few years older than me. I remember going to her sixtieth birthday party, when I was probably still in my early forties. I arrived, gave her a little hug and asked how she was doing.

As she embraced me she whispered, 'If anyone ever tries to convince you of the joys of getting old, they're lying. Being sixty is bloody awful.'

I guess she'd started drinking a little while before I got there. If I remember rightly she had her head down the toilet by eleven o'clock. But unshockable as I might now claim to be, I found that little aside decidedly unsettling. It didn't so much shock me as make me plain depressed. And now that I'm in my sixties myself I find I'm inclined to agree with her. Why spare the younger people? Why not just tell them the truth?

Actually, I once witnessed something which really did shock me – if not at the theatre, then at a graduation ceremony, which is just theatre by another name.

The son of some friends of ours was graduating at Oxford, so his parents and John and I drove up and went along to the ceremony before spending a few days in a cottage out in the Cotswolds somewhere.

Well, talk about tedious. Those must've been the most boring couple of hours of my life, which is saying something. It was in the Sheldonian – the building with what appears to be a selection of severed heads on the tops of columns all around the outside – and the whole ceremony, I kid you not, was in Latin, and consisted of nothing but an endless stream of students, in their gowns and mortarboards, shuffling through the place.

All we could do to try and stay awake was look out for our friends' son in that great black tide below us and to listen out for his name in the never-ending Latinate drone. Then, right at the end of the ceremony, when everyone got to their feet and started heading towards the exits there was a bit of a kerfuffle and I looked round and saw this woman on the gallery opposite us, who must have tripped and fallen. And somehow managed to go clattering down a couple of steps and bounce right under the railings. So that suddenly everyone in the building was watching this poor woman as she clung onto some post, with her skirt up round her backside and her little legs threshing about.

It was a good forty-foot drop below her. If she'd fallen, without doubt, she'd've broken her neck, and possibly taken out half a dozen graduates.

It was like the final scene of *North by Northwest*, where they hang off Mount Rushmore. Anyway, the people around her managed to grab a hold of her and slowly dragged her back up onto the gallery. It was only later that it occurred to me that somewhere below, in that great throng, was her son (it's funny, I never think of it being her daughter) watching, horrified. Which meant that from that day forward, whenever his degree came up in conversation the entire family would be quietly mortified, as they remembered poor Mum hanging off the railings and showing her knickers and flailing her legs about.

Anyway, that's quite enough writing (and drinking) for one day. I'm off to my (widow's) bed.

The wind is up. It's got all the dogs barking and the whole village is rattling about, with bits threatening to go flying off. It makes me appreciate just how exposed we are out here. It seems to be coming from the northeast, which might explain why it's so bloody freezing. A couple of hours ago that wind was picking up speed across Siberia.

I went out for a walk this morning. The first half was fine. I fairly flew along. I was wearing my big coat and felt pretty confident that if I leapt in the air and held my arms out I would've covered a good fifty yards or more. Coming back was more of a struggle and took at least an extra half an hour. I heaved into it with my shoulders, like a sumo wrestler. And found myself getting quite irate. At one point I got so worked up, I heard myself swearing into the teeth of the wind. Although who or what precisely was the focus of my ire was not immediately clear to me.

I've extended my little lease for another week or so. Hopefully by then I'll be right as rain. If not, I shall demand compensation. I shall sue.

Conjuring up a proper hot bath is still proving to be a gargantuan effort. I now have the heater switched on right round the clock, and when I feel the need to immerse myself in hot water coming upon me, I fill the kettle and put a pan on every hob. You should see that electricity meter spin.

But sooner or later there comes a point when you have to commit and actually turn the bath's tap on. The most I've managed is three lots of pans and kettles in with the bathwater. Any more is just too much traipsing up and down the stairs. This morning, as I stood over the cooker, waiting for the last round of pans to come to the boil, I began to wonder whether the water already in the bath wasn't actually cooling quicker than the water I was heating up.

It's like an ache. Or a sort of emptiness. I begin to see the sense in the wearing of black – a widow's weeds. It warns the rest of humanity that you're a-comin'. Like a bell or a big black flag. It also makes you look on the outside how you feel on the inside. Wretched. Bleak. Blasted. As if death is on you. Which I think it probably is.

If I was young I'd want to keep the old folks as far away from me as possible. You wouldn't want them around, reminding you how decrepit you may one day become. I'd herd us all up and drive us off the nearest bloody cliff.

I passed a couple of schoolgirls waiting for the bus this morning. They were chatting – about their hair and the advantages of having it long, because then you can do so many different things with it, and so on. I don't know how old they were. Fourteen or fifteen maybe. Two sweet little things, who'd obviously got up an extra hour early just so they could primp and prettify themselves. But they had that little glint in their eye, as if they'd only recently discovered this secret new currency and that, as things turn out, they were in possession of quite a haul.

I wanted to tell them to enjoy it. But to be careful. Not to put too much stock in other people's opinions, when it's based on nothing more than how you look. Because if you do and you begin to judge yourself and others by no better standard than how much interest you can stir up in men and boys, there'll come a day soon enough when you find your value slipping. And you'll begin to wonder where the hell you go from there.

What on earth they would've made of me I have no idea. Some aged old crow, no doubt. When I was a girl I remember having the nerve to ask one of my teachers – who seemed impossibly ancient – how old she was. She told me she was thirty-four.

Sometime in late November, about six weeks after John's death, I was walking home from the shops when I passed a youngish woman leaning over her buggy in which a toddler was having a bit of a gripe.

If I described the woman's hair as being lank or the sort of clothes she was wearing I could easily suggest what class she came from. But why bother? The fact is she was poor, or a good deal poorer than I am, and to all intents and purposes from an entirely different world.

She had her face right up to the child's face – a little trick which I'd soon discover was a favourite of hers. She might even have been swearing at the child. It doesn't matter. All that matters is that, as I passed, I happened to glance over, just as her little tirade was drawing to a close. The woman was straightening up. The child was clearly still quite cheesed-off. And, almost casually, as if to complete proceedings, I saw the woman take hold of the child's upper arm between her thumb and forefinger and give that infant flesh a sharp little nip.

The child burst into tears. Not surprisingly. It took me a moment to properly register what I'd just seen. I had to rerun it in my mind a couple of times, to be sure. But by the time I'd stopped and looked back, she was pushing the buggy behind me. And she must have had an inkling that I'd seen her, because she had her eyes on me.

I said something like, 'What on earth did you just do?' I may even have sworn. I've wondered more times than I'd care to mention, that if I *had* sworn, whether that would have been sufficient provocation and how things might have been different if I had not. So I might have said, 'What the hell did you just do to that child?'

The young woman stepped around the buggy and headed towards me. She was on me in no time at all. But it was the way she had a quick glance over her shoulder, to make sure that nobody was coming up behind us, that made me think that I was in trouble, and in that instant I felt all my moral outrage evaporate.

'And just what the fuck has that got to do with *you*?' she said, and jabbed me hard, just below the collarbone, for emphasis – a sharp little poke which I can still feel as I write this down.

And I knew straight away that she was quite capable of beating the hell out of me – and quite possibly killing me. I had this overwhelming sense of vulnerability. I found myself trying to work out how far I'd have to run to reach safety and where on earth that place might be.

I can't particularly remember the rest of our little exchange. I don't imagine I made much of a contribution. It consisted mainly of her telling me to mind my own fucking business, combined with a stream of quite personal insults. (Well, I suppose if you're going to insult somebody you might as well make it personal.) But as she carried on I had the distinct impression that she was working herself up into a state. As if, now that she'd finally found a legitimate target for whatever anger she'd been carting around all day, she might as well offload as much of it as she could. The longer her little rant went on, and the more I looked into her eyes, I had the sense that she was also gearing herself up for a small explosion of violence – a grown-up version of that little nip she'd just delivered to her child.

But just as she'd glanced over her shoulder before approaching me, I now saw her glance over mine. And I thank God that she must have seen someone coming towards us, because she suddenly stalled. Her little onslaught was suspended. And as a parting shot, she leaned right in towards me.

'I'll see you *later*,' she said, and jabbed me in my chest again.

Well, I scurried off up the hill just as fast as my little legs would carry me, and as soon as I got home I locked and bolted all the doors. And I didn't mention it to anyone for two whole days, and then only to Ginny. I think perhaps I was ashamed – at how frightened she'd made me. Like a bullied child, I'd thought that if I did actually tell anyone it would somehow only make things worse, to have things out in the open. And that by keeping it to myself I might somehow contain it. When, in fact, as I say, what I really wanted to keep secret was my shame.

When I finally spilled the beans Ginny insisted I go to the police and report the incident. And when I refused she appealed to my sense of morality – those same morals that had so quickly deserted me when that crazy woman stepped up to me. I should contact Social Services, Ginny said, because if she's prepared to treat her child like that in public, then how the hell might she be treating it behind closed doors?

All of which did nothing but make me feel even more awful. The truth is I was terrified of ever seeing the dreadful woman again. She'd looked into my eyes and known that she could trample all over me. So I made Ginny swear not to tell another soul and from that point on whenever she started haranguing me about it I'd immediately get all emotional, until she left me alone.

There's no doubt that if I'd had John around I wouldn't have felt quite so frightened. In the first instance, I'm sure, he would've flown off the handle and, just like Ginny, insisted I do something about it, etc. But at the close of the day when the lights went out he would've been there, in the dark, beside me. Someone for me to hide behind.

As it was, I became quite obsessed with her. And, as well as avoiding the street where I'd happened to encounter her, I drew in my mind a half-mile radius around it and created a no-go zone. Returning home from a bit of shopping I'd have a quick look all about me, to make sure she wasn't there, taking note of where I lived . . . just as I looked left and right before leaving the drive on my way out. And lying in bed, alone, I'd imagine her creeping round the garden, and trying the windows. Now just how screwed-up is that?

I managed to bestow on her a kind of omniscience. She

knew what I was thinking – was right there in my head with me. And the only solace I could find was that young policewoman who'd told me about John's death.

She'd be used to dealing with such people, I reasoned. She wouldn't be frightened. And in the midst of my deepest panics I'd comfort myself by thinking that if I was still half as terrified when I woke the following morning, I'd ring her up and tell her all about it – the equivalent of running to my mother and telling her how beastly some big girl had been to me at school. The obvious difference being that the policewoman was young enough to be my own daughter.

Rather contrarily, the other little scenario I sometimes envisaged was me going in search of my assailant. Finding out where she lived and stalking her for several days. And then, when she was least expecting it, I would leap out of the bushes and punch her square in the face. Knocking her senseless.

'How'd you like that?' I'd shout down at her, 'you disgusting little witch.'

Not a good day, by any means. Christ, and I'm not even halfway through it. Went into Holt to buy my Holbein. Things got off to a bad start when I bundled into the bookshop only to discover that David and Jenny, my future best friends, had been replaced by a young man in his twenties, who was engrossed in some weighty novel and looking very stern and full of himself.

To be fair, he could have been a happy, charming young fellow and I would've felt the same level of animosity towards him, since he'd wheedled his way into the role of second lieutenant that I had in mind for myself. Anyway, I very nearly asked after David and Jenny by name. Which would have made me look pretty stupid. I wonder how I would've got myself out of that little hole?

Then I went over to the Art section and looked high and low but couldn't find my precious Holbein. I kept thinking I must've got the wrong set of shelves, but I hadn't. Convinced myself that perhaps it had slipped down the back somehow and I started pulling out great stacks of books and piling them up on the floor. And I could see that young Johnny over at the counter suddenly wasn't quite so gripped by his bloody Tolstoy or Dostoevsky and kept peering over at me, to see what I was playing at.

I thought perhaps on my last visit I might've put it back

in the wrong place, i.e. unalphabetically. But I checked the whole damned section without the merest whiff of it. And I began to wonder if I'd perhaps hidden it away myself, in a secret location, to avoid anyone else buying it in the meantime, although I knew that that wasn't it. I even briefly imagined that the old duffer who'd asked about the picture on the wall – the chap that Dave and Jenny and I had all had a good old laugh at – had come back and, out of sheer spite, bought my Holbein, and was, at that very minute, feeding it, page by page, into the flames of his own little bonfire, and warming himself on my misery.

I should've just bought the bloody thing when I first saw it, instead of going through this stupid bloody ritual. I knew I wanted it. It cost next to nothing. True, I already have a perfectly serviceable edition of his prints at home somewhere, but I really did want a copy up here for my widow's cottage. I would've put it on the mantelpiece. It would've been a little talisman – a touchstone. And right now I need as many touchstones and talismans as I can possibly get.

I asked young Dostoevsky if he'd happened to spot it. He hadn't, but suggested that maybe someone had bought it since I last popped in. Well it was all I could do not to throttle him. But honestly, what exactly are the chances of one of the dozen or so people who've visited that shop in the last couple of days actually picking out my Holbein from the many thousands of books which line the shelves? And deciding to buy it? Unless it is indeed some awful cosmic conspiracy to try and make my life just that little bit more awful than it has been up to now.

I wandered around Holt in a state of quiet distraction. Of course, as soon as it became clear that I wasn't about to get my hands on that Holbein it was but a hop, skip and a jump to the absolute conviction that it was the only thing in this world that I wanted/needed. And I felt myself carrying around within me this Holbein-shaped hole. Without it I would be bereft. Hang on a minute! I'm bereft already. OK. It's not that my not having it would make me bereft. It's the fact that if I'd actually found it/bought it/owned it, some tiny fraction of my pain might have been erased.

And it's not as if just any old book of Holbein prints will replace it. Because now it is not about Holbein or even that particular edition, but that particular individual book. Well, I'm going to have to change the bloody subject, because this isn't helping. My point is that it needs to be the book that I saw the day before yesterday. And if it doesn't magically reappear in the bookshop in the immediate future, then I honestly don't know what I'm going to do.

To make matters worse I had a prang on my way home. Some of the lanes round here are so bloody narrow. I'd spotted another car coming towards me. So I did the decent thing and pulled over into one of those little passing places. And the arrogant bastard just flew straight by, without even raising a hand to say thank you. I must've been so annoyed, what with him and the bloody

Holbein, that when I pulled away I did so with just a hint of irritation and caught the nearside wing in the hedge. And when I reversed, to try and extricate myself, I was perhaps a little cavalier with my steering and I heard the distinct clunk of car making contact with something solid, hidden away beneath the foliage. And the more I went backwards and forwards and lost my temper the more scraping and squealing I could hear as the car rubbed up against whatever was in there.

When I got back to the village I didn't have the nerve to have a proper look at it. I just parked it right in the corner, with the damaged wing facing the bushes so that no one else could see it either. Perhaps if I leave it there long enough and do my best not to think about it, it might miraculously heal itself.

To try and calm myself down I went for a tramp out along the saltmarshes. I'd gone about half a mile before the whole path was blocked with bloody twitchers. I've spotted the odd one or two hanging about since I've been up here but today they were out in full force.

It's never struck me before but they really are a sort of ornithological paparazzi, with their telephoto lenses and their waistcoats with all the little pockets and sandwiches and their little fold-up stools.

As I squeezed past them I thought to myself, I am not going to ask what all the fuss is about. They're like children. It would only encourage them.

The other day, someone in the village told me how,

not that long ago, a bunch of birders gave some tiny bird they were chasing a seizure. It'd wound up in Norfolk by mistake and before you knew it word got round the twitching community and whole minibuses of them were spilling out onto the lanes. And they chased the little thing up and down the place with such determination that in the end its poor little heart just packed in. So they all had to climb back in their minibuses and go home again.

Apparently, the really rare birds that everyone gets so excited about are just an anomaly. They've been blown off course by some freak wind, so they're not even in pairs. Which means there's no prospect of them breeding, and no chance of them being blown back from whence they came. So they're just stuck out here, on the winter marshes of north Norfolk. A situation which has an eerie familiarity to it.

I seem incapable of stringing two decent nights' sleep together. Last night I was awake for a good couple of hours. As if what my body and soul need right now is a two-hour intermission to their slumbers. And, let me tell you, 3 a.m. in late January is a very lonely place to be.

I could have got up. It's meant to be better for you – to make yourself a cup of tea, or have a bath, or do more or less anything. I've forgotten the rationale behind it. Perhaps simply to prevent one's bed becoming fixed in one's mind as the place where one fails to sleep.

But there's not a lot for me to do round here. The TV's out of action. So it would just be more sitting around reading or staring into the fire. Writing these notes always feels like more of a daytime occupation. And, despite all the evidence to the contrary, as I lie in the dark I maintain a sort of deluded optimism that having just missed sleep's bus ten minutes earlier, another one will be along in no time at all.

I wouldn't particularly mind if lying there didn't inevitably seem to lead to me picking over all my anxieties, which then has a habit of slipping into an all-out panic attack. In my darkest hours I begin to think that nothing is connected. That every single thing on this planet is cold and blank and utterly disparate.

Last night, as I tossed and turned in my tiny bedroom, I remembered that odd little bedsit I had for my first couple of terms at college. It was on the first floor of a rather decrepit town house, with another two floors above it. And one night, when it was still warm enough to have my window open and the lights were out, I heard this odd noise come drifting in from one of the other flats.

It took me quite a while to work out what that sound was. Oh, innocent, innocent child! At first I thought it might be some animal, trapped or injured somewhere out in the garden. Or someone hurting somebody else. But it slowly dawned on me what was going on in one of the rooms above me. And, I won't lie, I thought it was just about the most thrilling thing I'd ever heard. I could hear the girl puffing and panting. Her little squeals of delight. And as the two of them carried on at it I could hear them talking – just the odd few words, about how much they loved each other. But, I mean, Hell's teeth. When was the last time I exchanged any sort of pleasantry whilst having sex?

Anyway, I was utterly spellbound. In fact, I was so entranced by the whole thing that I made the mistake of trying to open the window another couple of inches to get an even better earful. But the window must have squeaked as I tried to lift it. And all of a sudden the sound of the couple fucking ground to a halt.

I could hear them listening. There were one or two dark mutterings. Then I heard a window being firmly closed somewhere else in the building. And that was the end of that.

Sometimes, marooned in the middle of the night, I remember some of the men I slept with before John and I got married. Not that there were that many. Just a handful of encounters which took place a long, long time ago now. It's my own little archive of first-person erotica. And sometimes that's enough to get me off to sleep.

I really can't imagine anything worse than having a bunch of complete bloody strangers wandering round my home. And yet every year, in dozens of towns up and down the country, people throw open their doors and willingly surrender themselves to precisely such an intrusion when they have those dreadful Open Houses, and every Tom, Dick and Harry can come shambling in and admire the artistic endeavours of the home-owner who's half a term into an evening class in Watercolour at the local Tech. What really gets my goat is the way the weekend bohemians who host these things swan around the place as if they're bloody Velázquez, when the actual stuff that's up on the walls is about as sophisticated as a potato print. And it's perfectly clear that the only reason anyone's calling in is not to admire their gnarled lumps of pottery or home-made hats, but to have a gander at the size of the garden, or see what things look like with the sitting-room wall knocked through.

Perhaps I'm just plain antisocial. Certainly, I like to have some say over who comes and goes. All I know is that for those first few days after John's death it felt as if the house's fortifications had been breached and that I was overrun by the barbarian hordes. People were ringing and booking themselves in for a little visit. Others would just show up, unannounced. And they all needed to be fed and watered. Or at least to have their solemn half-hour in my company. My home became a sort of shrine. Until, after four or five days, at Ginny's insistence, I just let the phone ring. Then crept out at midnight and locked the front gates.

Putting aside the actual intrusion, I simply didn't have the strength to be dealing with other people's emotion. Not that they came around, I'm sure, with the intention of offloading all their grief onto me. They would just start talking and within a couple of minutes they'd fall apart. It was all quite genuine and heartfelt. But after it happened for the tenth or twelfth time I began to think to myself, What the hell am I doing counselling all these bloody people? I've got my own grief to be getting on with.

And, I must admit, I pretty quickly got pretty sick of hearing all the wonderful things people had to say about John. What a wonderful raconteur/good listener/generous soul he was. *Really?* I'd think to myself. *My* John? It was quite something to witness this man I'd known all my adult life being sanctified. And to such a degree that once or twice I was sorely tempted to point out a few of his less appealing habits. Not that it would've done any good.

And everyone had their own little story of when they last saw him and, in their own clumsy way, was determined to try and draw some significance from that final conversation. As if John had somehow known what was coming and had dropped something prescient, and even valedictory, into their exchange, regarding that new cheese shop up on Malden Street or the possibility of getting the house rewired.

But what I wasn't expecting – and, frankly, why on earth would I have been? – were the offers of sex. Five in all, and all five made within ten days of John dying. Two from close friends or relatives on John's side; the other three from husbands of friends of mine.

I've since had apologies from two parties. Mumbled, stumbling little speeches, with minimum eye contact – just like most apologies, I suppose – but neither one offering any real insight into their motives. I mean, were these offers made on a charitable basis? As a sort of little pick-me-up? Or should I conclude that all five of them had had their eyes on me for years? Had just been too polite to make a move whilst my husband was still living and breathing, but now suddenly saw me as fair game?

Who knows? In my kinder moments I'm inclined to think that it must just be some strange phenomenon born out of the circumstances. Sex being the only obvious refuge in the face of Death. And perhaps I'm not in a position to be too critical. All the same, allowing me to complete my first month's mourning might have been an idea. Just to show that they were, y'know, the *sensitive* type.

I've come up with a new way of eating, which I shall henceforth refer to as The Japanese Style. I guess it's just sort of evolved over the last few months, and these last couple of weeks in particular, and is down to the fact there's no one around to actually watch me eat.

Whereas I have always done the traditional eating-at-a-table and using-a-knife-and-fork routine, in London lately I found that I was just plonking myself down in front of the telly and eating my dinner off the coffee table. And up here in Widow's Cottage, I've got into the habit of just bringing the brim of the bowl right up to my mouth and gently shovelling in the necessary amount of food. Like the Japanese do when they're eating noodles. It makes much more sense if you think about it. Rather than the whole balancing-food-on-the-back-of-a-fork business, then lifting it up for a couple of seconds to see just how much falls off before delivering whatever's left into your mouth.

Some people might consider it simply slovenly behaviour, whereas I'm sticking with the Japanese thing. Of course, I wouldn't do it in public. But if no one else is around where's the harm? Who knows, I might start licking my plate clean. Or dispensing with cutlery altogether and just using my fingers. Or wiping my mouth on the cuff of my sleeve.

Actually, if I'm looking for somewhere to live, perhaps I should consider Japan? All that fish and rice is meant to be so very healthy. Someone famous once said that if you feel like a stranger in your own country, you might as well live abroad where feeling like a stranger doesn't feel so bad. Or something along those lines. I've never been to Japan (another good reason for going) but it does seem about as different from Britain as you can imagine. Except for the imperial past. And the island mentality. And the obsession with tradition.

Maybe that's not such a good idea after all.

Ginny's texts and messages have been steadily increasing in frequency ever since I got here. If I walk far enough out on the saltmarshes with my phone turned on it will suddenly have a little fit of bleeps and squeaks, as a backlog of communication finally finds its way through to me. So far I've done a stalwart job of ignoring them, but they've been getting more and more barbed and the text that reached me this afternoon simply said, 'ITD JUST BE NICE TO KNOW THAT YOURE NOT DEAD.'

That woman sure knows how to prick my conscience. So earlier this evening, having braced myself with a large glass of Semillon, I pulled on my coat and hiked out to the phone box, down by the quay.

It's been a long time since I visited a proper old-fashioned phone box. The door seemed to require an incredible effort in order to open it. Perhaps that's why we stopped using them? When she answered the phone and heard my voice she launched into a tirade of high sarcasm and bad language, which I allowed to just sort of wash over me until she managed to calm down a bit.

There was a short pause, whilst she got her breath back.

'Where the bloody hell are you, anyway?' she said.

I had a quick think before replying.

'East Anglia,' I said.

Another short pause down the line. Perhaps she was biting her tongue – telling herself not to be too hard on me.

'You couldn't be a bit more . . . *specific?*'

'Norfolk,' I said.

'OK . . .' she said, as if she was talking to a child now. Or a very stupid adult. 'And what are you doing up there?'

'I'm on the run,' I said. I was being more honest than she might have appreciated.

'Who from?' said Ginny.

'That's what I'm trying to work out,' I said.

I quite like the idea of me being some sort of fugitive. Someone who's considered potentially dangerous to the public. *Do not approach this woman. She's full of booze and ten different types of bitterness. And has a vile tongue on her. Call the authorities and we'll pop her with a tranquilliser dart – like we do the rhinos when they get out.*

Ginny and I talked, rather hesitantly. And at some point I asked, perhaps a little self-indulgently, what she'd been saying when people asked after me.

'Just that you're having a bit of a break . . .' she said.

For a moment there I thought she was going to say something else.

'Say the word,' said Ginny, 'and I'll come and get you.'

Again, there was something very appealing in the idea of me hidden under a blanket in the back seat of her car and Ginny sneaking me across the border.

A long pause whilst I turned it over in my mind.

'Are you ready,' she said, 'to come back home?'

For the first time in the conversation I found myself getting a little bit choked. I shook my head. Not that she could hear that.

'Not quite,' I said.

There was a long silence. Then Ginny asked me what it's like up here, at the moment.

'Wet and windy,' I told her. 'What's it like down there?'

I imagined her looking out of the window.

'Dark,' she said.

A little pause, all cold and empty. Then . . .

'I read a poem the other day,' she said. 'It made me think of you.'

OK. Now I was interested.

'Really? What was it called?'

I could hear Ginny thinking.

'I can't remember,' she said. 'It was in some anthology.'

And it transpired that she couldn't even remember what it was about – just that I would've liked it. So, now I'm always going to wonder about this poem. And become convinced, no doubt, that contained within those few lines of verse was some piercing piece of wisdom – a key to unlock the big bad door.

And, what with me wondering about this mythical poem, and Ginny trying to remember what it was about, our little conversation sort of fizzled out. I had this vision of Ginny sitting in her living room, surrounded by detectives wearing headphones, and tape recorders. The detective sitting nearest Ginny mouths the words '*Keep her talking*', as some sweaty telephonic expert fiddles with his hi-tech machinery.

'I've got to go,' I say.

'Really?' she says.

No. Not really. It's just that hearing her voice is making me feel funny. And not really helping me at all.

So we say our goodbyes. I tell her that I love her. And I hang up the phone.

The sweaty electronics expert is shaking his head. The chief detective's cursing.

'Another ten seconds and we'd've had the bitch.'

And I'm alone in my old-fashioned phone box, with a Siberian breeze whistling round my ankles. I stand there listening for a minute. Then I heave the door open, squeeze my way out of there, and head off into the dark.

I have bought myself a new car! Well, 'new' might be stretching credibility, but certainly *different*. It was parked outside someone's house with a For Sale sign taped in the window when I drove past it this afternoon. And being offered at what seemed like a very reasonable price.

It's yellow and Japanese – a nation who, as well as being healthy eaters are, I'm sure, car manufacturers of great repute. Before I'd even knocked on the door to the house I think I'd probably decided to buy it. The vendor – Alan – seemed quite nonplussed by my enthusiasm. Perhaps he'd expected me to haggle. I had a little sit in it and straight away it just felt much better, size-wise, than John's Jag, so we shook on it and whilst it wasn't a huge sum of money it's more than I tend to carry around with me, so I had to drive over to Sheringham to find a cash machine.

On the coast road, just over the brow of a hill, I went flying past a speed camera. Slammed my brakes on, as one does in such situations. But even as I did so I was thinking that there was something distinctly hinky about it. Something not quite right.

Sheringham itself is a town full of old men hanging about outside shops waiting for their wives and generally cluttering up the pavements. But on my way back I got a better look at the speed camera and laughed out loud when I realised. It's completely home-made. Apparently knocked up out of a few bits of plywood. Presumably, by some disgruntled local who's sick to death of cars speeding past the end of his drive. Something about the dimensions let it down – it's a tad too skinny. But the colour (probably the most important part of the deception) is quite convincing the same canary yellow as my new car, which, for some reason, I took as a good omen.

Alan had just counted out the money on his kitchen table and I was all ready to head off in my new car when he pointed out that I wouldn't very well be able to drive both cars back on my ownsome. To be honest, I was half inclined to just leave him the Jag. But Alan had a little think and told me that if I didn't mind waiting a couple of hours, he'd happily drop it round when his wife got in from work. And at the agreed time my lovely little car pulled into the village car park, with Alan at the wheel and his wife in the car behind him. I must say that as he handed over the keys I couldn't help but notice his missus staring at me, as if she'd been told about this crazy woman who goes round buying old cars without taking them for test drives or haggling over the odd fifty quid.

After all that excitement I decided that a little cat nap was in order and, for once, woke up feeling quite peaceful and rested. I have no idea how I achieved this. It seemed to have happened almost by accident. Even as I marvelled at my condition I fully appreciated that it wouldn't/ couldn't possibly last. That, within a matter of minutes, my old neuroses would re-establish themselves, etc. But it gave me hope that there might be a point sometime in the future when that sense of equilibrium might last for hours, even days at a time.

Ibought a couple of the Sunday newspapers this morning, primarily for the crosswords, but also to provide me with sufficient distraction on what has so far been a day of perpetual rain. Unfortunately, having had a first stab at the crosswords and a cursory flick through the magazines I made the mistake of pausing briefly at the Lonely Hearts section which did nothing to improve my mood.

I can honestly say I've never previously read, or even considered reading that particular section. And I can't come up with any reasonable explanation as to why I looked at it this morning. Curiosity, I suppose. And curiosity directed more towards the female entries, rather than anything to do with what was on offer, man-wise – perhaps just to see how the contemporary woman presents herself.

Well, I have to say that the news is pretty depressing. Despite the fact that most of the women are, by their own admission, in their forties, fifties and sixties the tone is relentlessly and exhaustingly upbeat. The word 'fun' jumps out from almost every entry, along with every possible variation, such as 'sparkly' . . . 'vivacious' . . . 'feisty' . . . etc.

To be fair, with only four lines in which to present

your case one can't help but be a little reductive. And I'm not sure quite what adjectives I'd use to describe myself right now. ('Unhinged' . . . 'desolate' . . . 'heavy drinker'?) But who in their right mind would kick off their list with 'Sexy'? Or even, excuse me, 'Foxy'? I was under the impression that foxiness had been laid to rest some time in the 1970s.

The entire page, it seems to me, smacks of desperation. Or worse, subjugation. The acronyms don't help. It eventually occurred to me that 'WLTM' in all likelihood stood for 'Would Like To Meet'. But 'TDH' . . . 'SOH' . . . 'LTR'? And 'GSOH'?? They remind me of those idiotic things we used to write on the envelopes of love letters, such as S.W.A.L.K. But in our defence we were probably about eleven years old at the time.

Euphemisms abound. 'Petite lady' is, I imagine, meant to imply '*on the short side*', but hints at being a little bit French. 'Rubenesque' presumably means curvaceous, and possibly even '*the larger lady*', but suggests that given the right circumstances she might be talked into lying naked on your settee. Sadly, in such exotic company, the few women who try to maintain a little dignity come across as simply frumpy. What, I wonder, is the shorthand for 'I have a PhD'? Possibly plain '*PhD*'. But I doubt that's going to fill your mailbag. Not when you're competing with women of the foxy and Rubenesque variety.

Romance, it seems, is not dead. It's merely dated. All country walks and fireside chats. Now, as I've already noted, I currently do a fair bit of walking. But I can't say the saltmarshes are exactly chock-a-block. Most days there are fewer than a handful of other figures between me and the horizon, which is just how I like it. Most people, I would guess, are probably at home, watching the telly. Or shopping. Or down the pub. I'm not making any judgement. People can do what they like. My only point is that when presenting themselves in a Lonely Hearts column people will always revert to what they think is expected of them. Clearly, people who read that page are looking for Romance. And what do Romantic People do? Go for Long Country Walks and have Candlelit Dinners. Followed, of course, by a Fireside Chat. Come to think of it, that pretty much sums up my day right now. Minus the Chat and the Candlelight.

Friends and acquaintances have recently begun to enquire, sotto voce, whether I might ever consider leaving myself open to meeting 'someone new'. The word 'companionship' is offered up, like some wafer of hope. But if all I'd wanted was a companion I'd stick to Plan A and get myself a dog.

I've witnessed Ginny and other single women discussing prospective partners and it's pretty discouraging. Within seconds the conversation turns into a pretty crude assessment as to what proportion of the man's hair and teeth remain. The implication being that, unless you make a supreme effort, or Lady Luck happens to be smiling down on you, you're likely to end up with something resembling a cadaver.

The funny thing is, if it'd been the other way around

and I'd gone first I'm sure John would've got remarried in next to no time. If anyone would've had him. And, strangely, I think someone would. John was one of those men who never quite understood women – he just knew that he needed one about the place. It wasn't even that he was incapable of doing the cooking and cleaning. No doubt in my absence he would've had a bit of a shock and probably appreciated me a little more. But within a couple of months he would have got to grips with most things. And the things he couldn't be bothered doing he would've paid someone else to do. Female company for him was simply an anchor. A point to fix his compass by.

Actually, I've just this minute worked out what LTR stands for. Presumably, Long-Term Relationship. Although I have to say that it's a little beyond me how anyone can make a public announcement that they are seeking an LTR with someone they've yet to meet.

A couple of days ago I was driving through a village just to the west of here and spotted what appeared to be quite a decent-looking restaurant in some old manor house. I pulled up at the gates, had a glance at the menu and thought that perhaps I was due a bit of a treat.

I've been eating an awful lot of cheese on toast/tins of soup lately. Admittedly, not a diet that's likely to kill me, but not likely to bring me into contact with many fresh vegetables either. Not unless you count the bits I occasionally spot floating in my soup. So yesterday I pulled on the boots I bought in Holt the day before yesterday and headed out onto the saltmarshes in the twilight, with my trouser legs rolled up, to stop them dragging in the mud, and a pair of smart shoes in my bag, to change into when I got there.

It can't have been more than about thirty or forty minutes before I was turning off the path and heading into the village and with just about enough light left for me to make my way. Then I slipped into the local pub and sat by the fire with my little pre-prandial and did the crossword for half an hour or so. So that by the time I tramped up the gravel drive to the restaurant it must have been about 6.30 or getting on seven.

I leant against a tree whilst I changed my shoes. There

wasn't any obvious thing to do with my boots, so I just tied the laces together and slung them over a drainpipe on the side of the manor house, and made my way towards the light. I hadn't bothered making a booking, what with it being a weekday in late January, and the girl at the door to the restaurant looked a little surprised to see me emerge from the dark.

'Just you?' she said. As if a single diner might not quite justify them waking the chef or turning on those great big ovens.

'Just me,' I said.

This provoked a good deal of fussing with the diary, despite the fact that not one of the twenty or so tables had anyone sitting at them. And when I declined her offer of a spot slap-bang in the middle of the dining room, like some bloody ornament, and requested a table by the window, there was even more consternation and flapping about.

To be fair, the food was perfectly fine – all stacked and drizzled in the obligatory manner. And I had two or three glasses of a Sancerre which smoothed everything out very nicely indeed. Eating on one's own can be a tricky business. The few times I've ventured out alone since John died I've taken a book along with me. As a rule, reading at the table is still considered to be bad form, but if you're on your own you do actually need something to occupy yourself or you're simply condemned to gawping around the room like an idiot or examining the tablecloth. It's not a problem when there's some food before you. It's all the waiting around in between.

I was about halfway through my duck confit when a couple came swanning in, him in his mid-forties and her a bit younger. I got the feeling that they were probably guests in the hotel, but this didn't seem to help put them at their ease. The British still haven't quite got to grips with the whole waiting-on/being-waited-on business. There is obviously untold cultural and emotional baggage stretching right back to the days of 'service', as well as all the usual hang-ups to do with class. Many waiters/waitresses are clearly uncomfortable being at someone else's behest, as if it's infra dig. And about the same proportion of customers, if not more, are so intimidated by the situation that they either tend towards a sort of awful fawning – as if they want to be best friends with the waiter – or overcompensate for all their insecurities and end up being plain rude.

By the time I'd finished my main course the bloke on the other table was getting his knickers in a terrible twist about how to pronounce 'roulade' or '*bois boudran*' and starting to take his embarrassment out on his girlfriend/wife. So I made the internationally recognised sign for 'Bill, please' – the mid-air squiggle – and got out of there just as fast as I could.

The moment I stepped outside the cold hit me. And it really was very, very dark. I had an old torch I'd found in the cottage, but had forgotten to bring a hat, so I headed off down the drive at quite a lick, just to try and get the blood pumping round my body and must have been a good five minutes out onto the saltmarshes when I remembered my hiking boots strapped to the side of the hotel.

I stopped – was sorely tempted to turn around and go back and fetch them. I stood there, dithering, in the cold and dark. Then I thought that if I didn't keep moving, with all that booze inside me, I might very well freeze to death. So I left my poor old boots to fend for themselves and vowed to retrieve them first thing in the morning, and pushed on with my nocturnal hike.

I once saw a list of all the lives lost on the mountains of the Lake District. And whilst one might be inclined to think that most deaths on, say, Scafell or Helvellyn would be due to people slipping and falling, I was rather startled to see the word 'benighted' attributed to so many of them. It's such a beautiful word, with such sinister associations. You stay out too late, or lose your way and slowly realise that the light is fading and that you're not going to have enough time to get home that night. You sit. The mist settles around you. The temperature drops and slowly drags yours down with it. You close your eyes and begin to slip away.

Well, I wasn't halfway home when the torch's beam began to wane. At first I felt reasonably confident that it would see me back, but within another couple of minutes the damned thing had conked out completely and the word 'benighted' began to rattle round my head. I stumbled on for a little way before it occurred to me that I hadn't the faintest idea where I was going. I turned around a couple of times, to try and get my bearings. There was no moon. No lights from any houses – or no obvious way of distinguishing those from a dwelling from something out at sea.

It was partly the drink, no doubt, but my head was now so cold it was as if it had been clamped in a vice. And I kept thinking of that point on the path where it suddenly drops by four or five feet, as it leaves the raised bank. So that I became convinced that I was about to go sailing off it and end up in a heap. And, all in all, I began to get myself in quite a state.

Darkness – real darkness – has a weight and texture to it. As if it might suffocate you. It seems ridiculous now, but I really did not have a clue how the hell I was going to find my way back to my cottage. It was as if I'd just been cast out into oblivion.

I was down on my hands and knees by this point. Couldn't tell whether the ground over which I was crawling was actually the path or just plain marsh. For some reason I'd removed my shoes – perhaps I was convinced I was going to lose them – and held one in each hand. Could feel my stocking feet and knees soaking up the wet as I crawled along. I carried on like that for quite a while. Like some animal, grubbing in the dirt. I was becoming increasingly freaked out by the situation. Was beginning to hyperventilate. Until, quite out of the blue, I felt this great ball of outrage rise up in me. There was no getting in its way. It came boiling up and quite overwhelmed me. And before I knew it I let out this almighty roar.

I really did make quite a racket. When I'd done, I let my head hang down between my shoulders, werewolf-style. Then I got to my feet, looked around, and made a snap decision as to which way was seaward, adjusted my course accordingly, and within two or three minutes saw the lights of the village up ahead.

When I finally got back under the streetlamps I began to appreciate just how much of the saltmarshes I'd brought back with me. But I held my head up as I marched back to the cottage. If anyone happened to encounter me they would just assume that I was some marshland monster. The same one they'd heard roaring ten minutes before.

Back home I changed, emptied a full scuttle of coal onto the fire and slumped in front of it. I kept nodding off, but was loath to go to bed until I was certain I'd warmed myself right through to my bones. And when I woke again it was about six o'clock, with me curled up on the sofa.

Actually, sleeping through till six is quite an achievement. But the first thing to enter my head was my poor old boots, still hanging from their laces on the side of the hotel. So I got in the car and drove straight over to the restaurant, without even having a cup of tea. I parked at the gates and went scuttling from tree to tree, to avoid walking up the gravel drive. Then there they were, still hanging on the wall like some weird piece of voodoo. And both of them covered in a fine frost.

They now sit propped up before the fire. The guilt still

nags away at me. Despite the fact that walking boots are meant to be particularly hardy and never happier than when they're out in the elements. I can't help but detect in their demeanour all sorts of trauma and resentment. In fact, I'm not sure I'll ever have the heart to take them out of doors again.

If it had been John that had had an affair I would've forgiven him. Which probably sounds terribly arrogant, or as if I'm just trying to let myself off the hook. I'm sure I wouldn't have been especially thrilled to hear about it, but the basic idea of him sleeping with someone else wouldn't have destroyed me in the way I think it would have done John if he'd heard I'd been playing around.

Of course, it's perfectly plausible that John did have an affair at some stage. That somewhere among the congregation at his funeral were any number of former lovers, each one crying her own precious little tears. But I doubt it. Not that John didn't take an interest in other women or, I imagine, cultivate his own little fantasies to get him through the day. And it's just about conceivable that some other woman on this planet might have felt herself attracted to the man with whom I shared most of my adult life. It's just that John was the kind of man who, having performed an act of infidelity, would've felt compelled to come running and tell me all about it. He was a bit of a baby like that.

All I'm saying is that if the situation had ever arisen I'm pretty sure that I would've forgiven him. There would have been a good deal of angst and a fair bit of shouting. But if it was clear that the whole thing was over then we'd've just gone limping on. Whereas, if John had ever found out about my little fling he would've left me. Of that I'm absolutely certain. It would've been the end of us.

Even now, I'm at a loss as to why I get so exercised about that bloody book on Holbein. I'm well aware that, on some level, it has nothing to do with the book at all. And that if I wasn't obsessing about Holbein I'd only be obsessing about how I seem quite determined to smash John's Jag up, which was, after all, his pride and joy. Or the fact that the blood blister under my thumbnail, where I trapped it in the bathroom, is slowly but surely taking on the appearance of a small black heart.

All the same, there really is something peculiarly beautiful about Holbein's portraits, and there's no question that they move me in some unfathomable way. Two or three of them I can remember quite clearly – namely, those on permanent display at the National Gallery. The most famous, *The Ambassadors*, is basically just a couple of fat guys standing around in all their finery, with a table between them on which a variety of spheres and measuring instruments have been placed. Each object, I don't doubt, is terrifically symbolic. But the painting's probably best known because of the hidden skull which is sort of smeared across the lower reaches and which you wouldn't necessarily notice unless you knew it was there. If you put your eye right up to the edge of the frame the skull suddenly jumps out at you. It's just a trick of perspective and, presumably, a little reminder about how we're all of us mortal and how in the long run none of our material wealth is going to be any use to us – a fact which, strangely, I don't need to be reminded of right now.

But that particular painting has never quite grabbed me. There's another one, of some woman in a woollen bonnet, with a squirrel perched on one shoulder and various crows and magpies bobbing about the place, which always puts me in mind of Snow White where she yodels out of the kitchen window and gets all the woodland creatures to come and help her with the washing-up. Beyond that, as far as I can remember, Holbein's output is just one long catalogue of kings and bishops and wealthy merchants – a cast of people not exactly guaranteed to set one's heart going a-pit-a-pat.

And yet I know that there is most definitely something about old Holbein that truly moves me. I remember getting tremendously excited by the backgrounds to his portraits, which are painted in these incredible turquoises and electric blues, and seem altogether too modern for the sixteenth century. But I'd like to think that there's a little more to it than that.

Something's happened to my hair. Something to do with the texture. It's sort of thickening up. Which I suppose is down to all the wind and salty air it's been exposed to. Either that or all the weird stuff going on in my head.

I can't say I mind that much. Just as long as it doesn't

end up getting all matted. Matted hair isn't particularly flattering on a woman of my age.

Having noticed it, it's crossed my mind on more than one occasion that woolly hair might be just another small step along the path towards me assuming the mantle of Wild Woman of the Saltmarshes. You know, the Anchorite look.

3.30 A.M.

How very disappointing. I'd been doing so well on the sleep front lately, and was under the impression that all those vaults buried deep inside of me, where my sleep is stored away, were gradually being replenished and that, inch by inch, I might be shifting from a state of near-capsize towards something more like equilibrium. But when I stirred half an hour ago I knew straight away that I was scuppered. And that if I carried on lying there I'd just end up tying myself in knots. So I thought I might as well get up and move about the place, and see if that did any good.

I'd made the mistake of thinking about the Holbein book again and how much I want to have it. Just to hold it. And, having fretted about that for a while, I remembered a fellow I once met at a dinner party, quite a few years ago now, who was a restorer and might even have been working at the National Gallery at the time. When I expressed some interest in his work he dipped a hand into an inside pocket, pulled out a small colour photograph and placed it on the table in front of me.

'Any idea what that is?' he said.

Of course, I hadn't.

'Caravaggio,' he said. '*The Way to Calvary.*'

The reason I didn't recognise it as a Caravaggio, or, for that matter, a figurative painting of any kind, was because the photograph consisted of nothing but a series of luminous gold and blue strata, like something chemical or even geological. Or a frame of film which has got caught in the projector, before burning up on the screen.

When he was satisfied that I was sufficiently bamboozled, he explained that it was actually a cross-section of the painting, viewed through a microscope, which he and his colleagues were analysing in order to identify the various pigments and layers of varnish and determine the precise order in which they'd been applied.

I'd never really given much thought to this notion of underpainting. And, to be honest, it took me a while to come to terms with the idea of someone slicing away at a Caravaggio, no matter how thin a sliver it might be. But as I listened to this restorer discuss his work I began to appreciate how a painting has a third dimension. And that, buried away beneath the surface, there might be an arm or leg which hadn't quite worked in the overall composition and had been painted out, but with the help of a little X-ray or infrared could be revealed. And how a painting which we now see as fixed and as if it could only ever have been precisely what it is might, in fact, have stray limbs and indeed whole characters swimming about beneath the paint.

And as I lay in bed, thinking about all those lost limbs and faces, I remembered something I must have heard on the radio twenty years ago, about someone who claimed to have devised a way of analysing a painting's individual brushstrokes so that they could extract from each one the words the artist had uttered at the moment the paint was applied.

Turning it over in my mind just now, I became convinced that the whole idea was utterly preposterous. And yet I distinctly remember hearing it. Or reading it in a magazine somewhere. I'm almost certain that it wasn't fiction – i.e. simply some speculation about what scientists might be capable of doing in years to come. I heard someone discuss, in all seriousness, the art of carefully lifting a single brushstroke and, from the tiny vibrations captured in it, identifying the words of Rembrandt or Vermeer or Raphael, just as if it were a piece of audio tape.

It seems that north Norfolk is in the grip of an outbreak of absent-mindedness. Like those inexplicable incidents of mass hysteria when hordes of adolescent schoolgirls collapse one after another in fainting fits.

A couple of days ago I was driving along some country lane and came round a corner to find a whole host of bits of paper strewn right across the road. You could tell that these were important bits of paper, with phone numbers on them, etc., and, being a civic-minded sort of person, I stopped and gathered them up – including a doctor's appointment card, a couple of folded five-pound notes and a pair of glasses – and took them along to the nearest police station. Judging by the state of the spectacles (i.e. aged and greasy) I'd guess they belonged to some doddery old fellow. I assume that he just liked to keep all his phone numbers and addresses in his specs case and was cycling along when they fell out of a pocket. Either that or he was abducted by aliens.

Then, less than an hour ago, I was marching through the drizzle to the Spar shop when I spotted some woman driving off with her handbag perched on the roof of her car. I had to flap my arms up and down as she drove towards me and was seriously considering throwing myself into the road. But when she finally stopped and

I explained the situation she seemed to find the whole thing unbelievably amusing. She couldn't stop laughing. Whereas, if that'd been me, I would've been beside myself. I would've had to go and lie down in a dark room for half an hour.

I'm pretty sure that neither incident would have bothered me half as much if I hadn't recently spent a couple of days up in the attic trawling through John's belongings and generally trying to sort things out. I'd gone through the clothes and shoes and so forth well before Christmas, which was its own particular nightmare. But these were his personal things – most of which hadn't seen daylight for a decade or more.

Christ, but what a hoarder that man was. There's something rather morbid, I think, about hanging onto every last little thing. I'm quite the opposite. I pride myself in my ruthlessness; my lack of sentimentality. If it'd been my own stuff most of it would've gone straight into the recycling. But as it was John's, and what with him being so recently dead, it wasn't so easy and it's very hard sometimes to know where to draw the line between what's of any sort of significance and what's not.

There were stacks of mags, including some of a 1950s boxing variety, in various bundles and tied up with string, which all went straight to the charity bookshop. There was a great stack of archaic photographic equipment and slide projectors, which I put aside for one of John's old cronies who's into that sort of thing and who can decide whether or not they're any use to him. It was all the personal papers and documents that were the problem.

To be fair, John probably hadn't planned on dying when he did do. Perhaps he'd envisaged many a long evening in his dotage sitting up in the attic, getting all misty-eyed surrounded by boxing mags and his old cricket whites. The problem is, whatever I fail to dispose of now will only be disposed of later by some complete stranger. We never had kids. When he wanted them I didn't, then vice versa. And by the time we were finally in accordance it was pretty much too late. I only note that here because when I'm gone there'll be no one with heavy heart sifting through all our combined junk. And even if there was, most of it wouldn't mean anything to them. Most of it doesn't mean that much to me.

I occasionally wander round some saleroom, on the lookout for an old rug or piece of furniture, and there will always be several dozen cardboard boxes, full of letters and photographs and so on, usually labelled 'Ephemera'. It's just stuff that's been dredged up along with everything else in some anonymous house clearance. But some of these things are deeply personal and private. That photograph of four men in the 1940s, posing on some unidentifiable beach in their big trunks with their arms around each other's shoulders – to someone, somewhere that photo will have considerable emotional weight. Just not for you or me.

But it's a salutary lesson. Personally, I shall be leaving strict instructions regarding exactly how big a bonfire to build. The alternative is surrendering your most intimate possessions to some man with a van, called Steve or Gary. And the prospect of a crowd of strangers rummaging through your most personal mementos one Saturday morning. And that really does make me feel rather queasy, I have to say.

I never told a soul. Not even Ginny. Which is probably a fair measure of the scale of the deceit, because ordinarily I tell Ginny just about everything. Whether she wants to hear it or not.

To be perfectly honest, since John's death there have been a couple of occasions when, after the third or fourth glass, I've been tempted to blab about it. But I've always managed to stop myself just in time. I've instinctively known, I think, that I'll regret it – either the next day or the very next minute. It's as if, when John was still alive, I'd made a vow to keep it to myself, and that spilling the beans now that he's gone would be unfair on him. Of course, it could just be me covering up my shame. Not the shame of the actual affair (of which there isn't much to begin with) but the way that it ended. Maybe there's something in that.

In fact, Ginny should probably shoulder some of the responsibility. It was, after all, her who browbeat me into signing up for the short course at Dartington Hall in the first place. And if she hadn't backed out at the very last minute because of some drama with her current beau, then she would've been there, like my very own chaperone, and that would've been that.

I was tempted not to bother going myself, but finally

decided to make the effort. The course was fine. One or two of the sessions weren't particularly inspiring, but there you go. I'm pretty sure I'd seen Paul around the place, though that could just be me investing some sort of significance after the event. But on the last night I definitely noticed him. There was a ceilidh in the Great Hall. And whilst we didn't actually bump into each other amongst all the do-se-dos and stripping-the-willows, I do remember glancing over at him once or twice and seeing him watching me.

The whole thing was drawing to a close and the band had struck up the opening bars of 'Auld Lang Syne' or something equally maudlin, and I've always been deeply allergic to that sort of forced sentimentality, so I headed for the door. I've tried a hundred different times to remember exactly what was going through my mind as I made my exit. Whether I felt any sense of disappointment at not having spoken to him or just how much of an impression he'd made on me. And I honestly can't remember. But from that moment on it's as if everything is carved in stone.

Between the Great Hall and the quadrangle there's an old porch, like a church porch only bigger. And when I stepped through the wooden door into it I found him sitting there. I wasn't even aware that he'd left the hall. I pulled the door to behind me and as I passed, happened to glance over at him. He said, 'I'm sorry for staring. But you're just about the loveliest thing I've ever seen.'

I carried on walking. Down the stone steps, and headed

across the quadrangle, towards the door which led up to my room. I made it all the way across the lawn. Was standing at the door, with the key in my hand. It was like some sudden, debilitating sickness. As if, within those fifty yards or so it had taken hold of me and struck me down.

I've often wondered if it was something to do with the way he said it. I feel quite sure that if he'd been smirking or even smiling then that would've been the end of it. But he wasn't. The words seemed almost sad.

I was still standing there in the doorway, with that stupid key in my hand. I was having trouble breathing.

'Jesus Christ,' I said. My heart was pounding. Then I turned and headed back across the lawn.

It makes no significant difference how long there was between me walking back over to him and talking to him and the two of us being up in my room and on my bed, screwing. Whether we chose to go straight upstairs, or spent half the night wandering round the gardens, quoting poetry at each other by moonlight as some sort of preliminary. The fact is that as soon as I turned away from the door I knew that we'd be sleeping together. That decision had been made.

I'd had a couple of drinks but was barely even tipsy. I knew what I was doing. I wasn't taken advantage of. Even so, it might well be that the fact that we were both on our own and far from home might possibly have contributed somehow. That, in effect, there was nothing to connect whatever went on that night down in Devon to our lives back home. And that, if we'd chosen to, we could have remained quite nameless. Like some perfect little crime.

But within about five minutes I'd decided that, whatever this was, one night of it was not going to suffice. Not by a long chalk. And before the sun was up the following morning I was already plotting to make sure it didn't slip away from me.

I can clearly remember sitting on the train the next day in a state of absolute distraction, not least by my newfound loveliness. Apparently, this young man, fifteen years my junior, had identified it, buried so deeply in me that I wasn't even aware of it myself. As that train dragged me back towards London a great many things went through my mind, one of which I particularly remember. And I'm well aware just how supremely selfish this is going to sound. I kept thinking, 'Whatever this is, how can it be anything other than a good thing?' And not simply because it was providing me with so much unalloyed joy. It was as if my very spirit had been plugged into a whole new universe of goodness. Everything around me was transformed. The world was kinder. Dammit, the world was downright wonderful. And how could that possibly be a cause for regret?

Popped into the letting agents this morning and basically told them I'd let them know when I was moving out. If anyone's desperate to rent the place in the meantime, they can call round and we'll take it from there.

At this rate I might as well just buy the place and have done with it.

There seem to be an awful lot of dead animals at the side of the road up here, which is pretty depressing. But I suppose dead rabbits, etc., are bound to be a bit more prevalent in rural Norfolk than NW3.

John had a theory regarding roadkill – or, more specifically, to do with the number of them one encounters in the country – the essence of it being that whilst it's all very sad seeing the corpse of, say, a badger, one can at least take some comfort from the fact that this must be but a small proportion of the overall population and that the more flattened badgers one sees the more living, breathing variety there must be, out in the woods.

Another little theory he was fond of espousing when we were driving down country lanes had something to do with the number of dead insects hitting the car's windscreen and how the lack or abundance of them related to the local use of pesticides. It was only marginally different from the dead badger theory and I sometimes wheel it out to give people an idea what level of conversation I've had to put up with all these years. Anyway, the first one – the roadkill theory – came to mind when I was out in my new little car a couple of days ago and drove round a bend to find something flapping about in the middle of the road.

It took me a second to work out that it was a pheasant. Must have just been clipped by a passing car. Either one of its wings was broken, or it had taken a blow to the head, because it was making a terrible, bustling fuss. Now, anyone who's observed a pheasant at close quarters will appreciate what an incredible void of intelligence is contained therein. I know strict vegetarians who can't quite muster umbrage at the prospect of the poor buggers being shot at, despite the fact that the only reason they're actually airborne long enough for someone to shoot them is because someone else has just chucked them up there the second before. But seeing it squawking and hobbling about the road made me feel quite ill. The poor thing was clearly in some distress.

There wasn't enough room for me to drive around it, even if I'd wanted to. And it's not as if I felt remotely qualified in approaching it, getting a hold of it, or any other thing. Luckily, a car coming the other way stopped – some chap jumped out and went striding over towards it. And in a flash he took the bird up in his arms and carried it over to the boot of his car. Then he jumped back in and even waved at me as he went on his way.

Thank goodness, I thought. Thank goodness these country folk know what to do in such situations. But it was a good couple of minutes before I began to question the speed with which he'd managed to get the injured bird to calm down. And it slowly dawned on me that perhaps he wasn't actually driving it off to pheasant hospital. That, in fact, when his back was turned to me, in all likelihood he just gave the bird's neck a quick twist. And that he was now taking it home with the intention of hanging, cooking and eating the thing.

I have this idea sometimes that John is alive and going about his business – in the next room, or a neighbouring town – quite oblivious. As if there's been some administrative oversight or clerical error which has somehow kept us apart.

Quite often, when the phone goes my first thought is, 'That'll be him . . .' Or, 'I was wondering when he was going to call.' Or I'll just be pottering around the house and become aware that there's someone I really must get in touch with. And for that first fraction of a second I'll not know who it is I'm thinking of. Then, Oh yes. That man. That husband. The one I lived with for forty years.

Going home to John after that first little infidelity was, it transpired, to be no great stretch on my part. Which is to say that I was neither riddled with guilt nor seized by some overriding need to unburden myself and tell him what had gone on. All I did, in effect, was slip back into a role I'd been perfecting over the previous twenty-five years. Or, to put it another way, I drew around me the plain grey vestments of domesticity and disappeared from view.

When asked about the course, I reported that it had been fine, but that one of the tutors had not been quite as rigorous as one might have expected. (True.) Asked if I'd made any friends, I talked at length about a woman with whom I had indeed been rather pally, but made her out to be a good deal smarter and more entertaining than the real-life version, so that her towering wit and personality eclipsed everything else.

My point, I suppose, is that no real subterfuge was necessary. If our marriage at that time could in any way have been considered a success it was in the fact that each of us gave the other sufficient leeway to get on with their life. Most days of the week we had breakfast and supper together and probably spent half of the week's evenings in each other's company. But we were hardly inseparable.

I'd arranged to ring Paul the following day and, in order to avoid having his number appear on any future phone bills, I walked over the Heath and popped into the phone box on Gilmour Street. I can't remember very much about that first phone conversation, but I distinctly remember saying that I missed him, despite the fact that I'd only met him a day or two before. And I clearly recall that, along with every conversation that followed, we rarely, if ever, mentioned John. I'd told Paul that I was married within five minutes of our meeting. But after that it was barely referred to. We probably felt we had other, more important things to be discussing. Though, whatever they were and however important they seemed at the time, most of them have since just slipped away.

What is also crystal clear in my memory is how whenever I walked up over the Heath towards the phone box I had that same knot of excitement in my stomach. I became increasingly light-headed. I became upset. Then I'd finally pull the door to behind me and dial his number – originally written on the back of an old till receipt, but memorised within days in case I happened to lose it – and Paul would pick up. And I'd practically be in tears, I was so happy. And we'd talk for half an hour or so. Then, at the end of each call, we'd arrange when I'd call him next, and for the days that followed that would be my whole life's focus – the only thing that mattered to me.

Only once, as I remember, was the phone box occupied when I arrived at it. Some old girl who, when she happened to see me waiting, turned away to shield herself from me. I doubt I had to wait more than a couple of minutes. But it was long enough for me to half lose my mind. As if that phone only connected to one particular house in Norfolk, or Paul would not be prepared to wait an extra minute or two. So that when the old trout finally surrendered the phone box and I dialled Paul's number and it rang for a little longer than usual I honestly thought that the only good thing in my life had been snatched away from me.

We would've met up again a good deal sooner but John and I were booked in to visit some friends out in New England and, barring me faking an aneurysm, there wasn't much I could do to wriggle out of it.

I must have thought to myself a hundred times that week, 'Christ, but these people are so *dull* ... their jokes so *lame*,' etc. When I look back now my behaviour is not much different from a moody teenager – albeit one entombed in the body of a middle-aged woman. Our hosts would suggest a drive up into the mountains. *Boring.* Or a trip down to the lake. *You're kidding me.* I'm only surprised that someone didn't take it upon themselves to try and slap some sense into me. And all the time I kept thinking, None of this matters. Because in another week or two I'll be with someone who truly understands me. And that allowed me to rise above the dreariness of my dull, dull husband and our dull American friends.

Unfortunately, on one occasion I managed to make an absolute fool of myself when Jay, one half of the couple with whom we were staying, made some little joke at John's expense. He was just ribbing him about something or other – about him getting old or how scruffily he was dressed. And I suddenly went storming in to John's defence, and gave Jay a terrible ear-bashing. When I finally stopped, to catch my breath, I remember looking round and seeing all three of them staring at me, open-mouthed, as if I was a complete bloody lunatic.

I don't know how long it took me to work out that, in fact, the object of my wrath was a little closer to home. Because whatever Jay had said in jest I had obviously been considering a good deal more seriously. On two or three occasions I'd already found myself sneaking a peek at John out of the corner of my eye while we were watching telly – noticing how his hair was becoming thin and fibrous. Or the little network of broken blood vessels on his cheeks. If I'd noticed them before they'd never particularly bothered me. But now I had someone to compare John to. And making comparisons like that, without the person knowing, is a mean little trick to play.

I've never had that many friends. I guess I'm just not a people person. If that's the case, I have to say it doesn't bother me. To be honest, I'm deeply suspicious of anyone who claims to have hundreds of chums and whose every utterance begins with, 'My friend Sally . . .' this or 'My friend Caspar . . .' that. As if the only reason for these poor souls' existence is to be considered in relation to this one exceptional individual, like tiny planets orbiting some mighty sun.

I could count on the fingers of one hand those people I consider to be my real friends, i.e. women with whom I have an absolute affinity and whom I wouldn't think twice about calling up in the middle of the night (a theory I've recently put to the test). Beyond that, I suppose, there exists a light scattering of acquaintances – people whose paths will occasionally cross my own – who are perfectly pleasant, but I wouldn't for a minute consider play a significant role in my life.

I'll sometimes find myself in mid-conversation, having agreed to go round to someone's house for a coffee, and think to myself, 'What the hell am I doing sitting here listening to this drivel?' And it's all I can do not to get up and say, 'I'm sorry, I've made a terrible mistake,' and head for the door. But, of course, one just sits there, enduring and even perpetuating what must qualify as one of the world's most tedious conversations, knowing that you're not actually about to do a runner, which only makes things worse.

It's not quite the same I know, but once or twice lately I've been politely chatting with someone and have had this peculiar impulse to do something quite drastic, even violent. There's this old dear who has lived on our road since the Iron Age and knows everybody for miles around. She's not a gossip. In fact, I doubt there's a malign bone in her body. But I bumped into her in a local teashop and she was being so sweet, and I was being so sweet back to her, and after a couple of minutes of this I had a powerful urge to just punch her on the nose.

Of course, this is a little different from people not being sufficiently interesting. In fact, I suspect that it's bordering on clinical psychosis, which rather worries me. If I was being super-rational I might say that perhaps it's me wanting to show that despite the calm little scene that we've created there's actually all this rage and chaos bursting to get out. And that everything is very far from being all right. But I know that if I did actually sweep all the crockery off the table, or grab the old dear by her hair and start swinging her around the place, then in no time at all I'd be carted off to some remote institution, and that wouldn't agree with me at all.

Years ago, when I was still in my twenties, I was on a train heading up towards the Lake District and this young French girl got on and sat down opposite me, and we got chatting and she told me about this amazing trip she was having, right the way across Europe, long before such a thing became quite common, let alone for a young girl on her own. Anyway, she really was quite charming and at some point she produced this little notebook with an elastic band round it which was crammed with bits of paper. And she told me how it contained the names and addresses of all the wonderful people she'd met on her travels, which meant that she could pitch up in just about any city in Europe and know that she'd have a place to stay.

A little while later she went off to the toilet and I was left staring at this precious book on the table before me. And I had this dreadful compulsion to get a hold of it and fling it out of the window. Really, I had an awful struggle. I mean, she must have spent a good five minutes saying how she'd simply die if anything happened to this book, then went off and left it right in front of me, as if I'd been set some great moral test.

Of course, I didn't actually fling it out into the fields of Warwickshire or whichever county we happened to be travelling through. But that strange urge certainly unsettled me. And I've sometimes been inclined to think that it was because she was living the bohemian life that I coveted for myself, and that I simply wanted to punish her for that, and for being so condescending. But the truth is she wasn't remotely condescending, and the only possible explanation is because I knew it was exactly what I was not meant to do.

By the time we got back from New England I was quite beside myself and desperate to see Paul again. The actual flight seemed to take forever. Took so long, in fact, that I had a rather odd little episode when I became convinced that I was going to be stuck up in the sky indefinitely, somehow caught between time zones, and had to put my head between my knees to calm myself down.

I finally caught up with Paul the following Tuesday, in Cambridge. John was away for the day, at a meeting at the other end of the country, and wasn't due back till last thing at night. So the moment he was out of the house I jumped in the car and hammered up the M11 and must've been there by ten or eleven o'clock.

It seems a little tawdry now to talk about hotel rooms, and paying in cash, and our deliberations regarding whose name and address to write in the register, etc. But at the time it didn't feel remotely tawdry. They were just the means necessary to avoid any complications which could make life difficult for us in the future. If the woman behind the desk had happened to raise an eyebrow, or even picked up on some disparity in our ages, then I didn't notice. And even if I had it wouldn't have troubled me one jot.

I just wanted to get Paul upstairs and into bed. Not because I was some terrible whore, but because I felt so passionately about him. What he felt for me I'll never know. No one ever really knows what someone else is feeling, no matter how honestly that person might try to articulate it. Quite often I find that, years after the event, I interpret my own motivations quite differently anyway. So if you can't say with any certainty what's going on inside yourself, how can you expect anyone else to know?

Well, we bundled ourselves up into our room, pulled back all that clean white linen and ripped each other's clothes off. After we screwed we lay in the bath and talked for half an hour. Then screwed some more. And, having worked up a bit of an appetite, we dressed and ate at that Italian place in the corner of the open market.

Paul knew Cambridge a good deal better than I did so he led the way down by the colleges, and out into a sort of meadow, with all these cows wandering up and down. And we walked along in that wonderful stretch of wild land, less than half a mile from the city's spires.

If I ever feel the need to torment myself with how incredibly happy I once was – and it's a habit I seem surprisingly fond of – then it's that little scene that I tend to return to. The two of us just walking along in the autumn sunshine, with a chill in the shadows, which just makes you appreciate the heat all the more. I felt so good and things seemed so light and bright and full of possibilities that when I look back now I'm almost embarrassed. Actually, to be fair, it's not that I'm embarrassed. I just sort of cringe at my blind optimism, which one might easily excuse in a schoolgirl, but not a woman just shy of fifty years old.

I left it as late as possible before heading back to London. Which meant that I ended up haring down the motorway almost as madly as I'd hared up it twelve hours before. I was flying along at God knows what sort of speed and still some way short of the M25 when the driver of the car in front of me suddenly slammed his brakes on and I came within a whisker of going smack-bang into the back of him.

It was one of those moments that as soon as it's over you almost pass out from all the adrenalin. And as the traffic slowly started moving again I had this vision of me having to explain how I'd come to have a crash halfway up the M11 when I'd claimed to be meeting some friends in town.

The only other thing of note we did that first full day together was drive out to the American Military Cemetery, at Paul's suggestion. I remember thinking that a cemetery didn't sound particularly romantic. But Paul insisted that I was going to love it. So there – he must've wanted to impress me. To show me something that was important to him.

The American Cemetery is on top of a hill a couple of miles west of the city, with the same acres of crosses and headstones as most other military cemeteries. The same shocking uniformity. It's the chapel that sets it apart. Just a large rectangular room – quite monolithic-looking from the outside – with a high ceiling. But light and modern. I wouldn't know when it was created. The 1950s, I suppose. Inside, cut into one wall, is a vast map of Europe, with all these metal planes fixed to steel rods radiating out from East Anglia across the continent. In the windows opposite are all the emblems of the different US states, in stained glass. But it's when you look up that it really hits you. The mosaic across the ceiling is a combination of angels, with their arms raised above their heads, flying in formation, alongside bombers.

It sounds quite crass, the way I've described it. In fact, there is something almost naive at work, which helps make it so moving. And it struck me then, just as it struck me when I visited the cathedral of St John the Divine in Manhattan, where tiny baseball players are incorporated into the stained glass, that we would never dare do such a thing in England. Not in a holy building. Except at a place like the Military Cemetery out at Madingley, which is, after all, just a small corner of the United States in Cambridgeshire. And as I stood there looking up and all around me I thought to myself, John would never be able to appreciate the beauty in this. Not in a million years.

Spent most of this morning wandering around the sands out at Holkham. I parked up on that wide drive just off the coast road and found a sandy path that zig-zagged through the fir trees and came out behind the dunes. My original plan had been to walk out to the sea and have a little paddle, but the water was nothing but a thin, silver line on the horizon, so I decided just to have a stride around.

Christ, but it's a big old beach. I'd forgotten. The sort of place where you could imagine someone attempting a land speed record. I walked up and down, trying to find the spot where Paul and I had sat, however many years ago that is now. It was autumn, but still quite warm. We must have sat there for hours. Some part of it, I'm sure, we spent kissing, and quite possibly groping each other. We may even have talked from time to time. But the majority of it we just sat there, curled up together, with Paul's coat wrapped around us. Huddled under the firmament, with the roar of the sea somewhere way off in the distance.

If I think about it long enough I can retrieve some tiny fragment . . . some tangible taste of what was going on inside of me. And the best description I can come up with is that it was as if the world was suddenly a very good place to be. That I belonged here. And that, up to that point, I'd been making my way through my life on little more than a fraction of my capacity.

Well, I had no luck this morning trying to find the spot where we'd been sitting. I always thought that we'd been due north of a series of sand dunes. But I must've marched up and down for a good hour and a half without seeing any sign of them. I suppose it's possible that the landscape has somehow changed in the meantime. Sand does, after all, have a tendency towards transformation, especially when it's exposed to the wind. Then again, it's not exactly the bloody Sahara. And it's much more likely that I was just on the wrong part of the beach.

Not being able to find that particular spot quite upset me. I'd wanted very much just to sit there again and see if I could pick up some trace of that benevolent power. And not being able to do so had me wondering if it was possible that I'd made the whole thing up.

That same weekend we were walking along a lane a couple of miles inland and saw this great V of geese flying overhead. Then another one. And within a couple of minutes that huge blue sky was strewn with thirty or forty of these squadrons of geese – way, way up above us. And it was so still that we could clearly hear the sound of their wings pumping away at the air.

When you're in love – or infatuated or besotted or whatever you want to call it – moments like that are a sort of benediction. My fear now, and it's a real fear, is that when I encounter anything with even half as much wonder, what will I do with it? In the past, if I happened to be alone when I witnessed something magical I always knew that I'd be seeing John later and I'd be able to report it back to him, which, in its way, still served to validate the experience. Even if it was just some eccentric little thought I'd had. But now I worry that without someone else to share my thoughts with, all the magic will just drain away.

I thought it would help, being out on the beach. Thought it might recharge my battery. But, if anything, it's just made things worse. And by the time I'd spent a couple of hours flailing about I felt so low that I just got back in the car and drove around, to try and distract myself. To try and clear my head.

At some point there was a programme on the radio, about a group of women who were being referred to as War Widows, but not in the conventional sense. So many young men lost their lives in the Second World War that when it was finally over there were simply not enough of them to go around. It's one of those facts that is so blindingly obvious only after someone else has pointed it out to you. Strange also that that generation would have included my mother, but I never heard her make any reference to it.

Anyway, they interviewed some old girl who was talking with great stoicism on the subject, as if life was just some dance down at the local Alhambra or Locarno and if you were lucky some fellow might happen to come along and invite you out onto the dancefloor. But, what with there being twice as many girls as boys, she never got the chance. Of course, her resilience just made it all the more moving. And to my shame I found myself thinking that perhaps if you never happen to find a partner, you never miss what you've not had. Honestly, sometimes I surprise myself with my callousness.

And then the strangest thing happened. I was just puttering along down some country lane when this man – I couldn't even say how old he was – but this man of indeterminate age crossed the lane before me, barefoot, then climbed a stile into a field.

I carried on down the road, thinking, He's probably just strolled off the beach. But then it occurred to me that we were nowhere near the beach here. That we must've been the best part of five miles from it. Not to mention the fact that it was the middle of winter. Then I felt this awful sense of doom creep up my back and sweep across my shoulders – a sickening sense of everything suddenly being quite wrong.

I pulled up and reversed the car to the point where I'd seen him. And when I stopped by the stile there he was, halfway across the field. I was tempted to get out and call after him. To ask him what was with the bare feet. He would've almost certainly heard me. But some van came up behind me and started honking his horn, so I had to carry on.

And like everything else these days if I allow it, that merest glimpse of a barefoot man has been niggling away at me ever since. As if there's something askew. That there is inexplicable strangeness and peculiarity all around me.

And perhaps even some terrible conspiracy.

All afternoon, whenever I thought of him I kept thinking of a dead man. That's what bare feet mean to me. And that's not just me being loopy, surely? Think of all the to-do when Paul McCartney was photographed walking barefoot across the zebra crossing on the cover of *Abbey Road*. A man with bare feet signifies death. Everyone knows that.

And I began to think that if I wasn't careful the bare feet would join the Holbein and the black heart under my thumbnail and all my other little obsessions, over which I expend an inordinate amount of mental energy, which I can frankly ill afford. Then, only an hour or so ago, it suddenly dawned on me. I suddenly worked out what was going on. That not far from where I passed the barefoot man is Walsingham – that little village with all the shrines and springs. The man I saw was, in all likelihood, a pilgrim. He was walking barefoot, the last mile of the way.

It's an odd sort of word. *Widow*. I keep trying it on for size – *widow's weeds . . . widow's walk . . . widow-woman* – but can't say I'm especially enamoured. Rather vainly, I don't consider myself sufficiently wizened. On the other hand, *widowhood* – that period of indefinable length which I have apparently now entered – sounds rather inviting. It conjures up a black cape or cloak, with a good-sized hood on it. Like Meryl Streep in *The French Lieutenant's Woman*. Actually, I think I'd look pretty good, wending my way across the windswept marshes. Although, all that billowing material would be bound to slow you down.

One of the major downsides to cohabitation is the fact that you can enjoy the most wonderful day and be pretty much skipping around the place, only for your partner to arrive home after the most appalling of days and within a minute all that *joie de vivre* has been squashed underfoot.

It's just a law of physics, or possibly chemistry, that if you introduce one element to another, and one of those elements has had an insufferably crappy day, then the crappiness always comes out on top.

It used to drive me mad. In fact, I would sometimes insist that John had an hour or so to himself when he got in from work, just to calm down or acclimatise to the domestic environment. Or I would simply disappear into another part of the house where he couldn't find me and hope that by the time we next met up he wouldn't be quite so pissed off with the world.

Of course, since John's death my thoughts on the matter have had to be amended slightly. If I wake up in a funk now, or manage to develop a certain crotchetiness during the day, my only option is to wait for it to pass, like bad weather. Either that or try to analyse it into oblivion, which is often too tedious to contemplate. There is no one around now, or due home, to whom I can kvetch and moan in an attempt to alleviate my grumpy load. Not unless I've previously arranged to meet someone at some point during the day (or hastily done so with that sole intent). But even moaning to a friend is not the same as moaning to your husband. One doesn't feel any sort of guilt making one's husband a little bit miserable. That's what they're there for. In fact, in all sorts of ways once you've been together for a couple of years you begin to treat your partner with the same level of contempt previously reserved for yourself.

I didn't set out to pay a visit to Walsingham – at least, I don't think so. I just happened to be over at Burnham Market and on my way back spotted a sign to the village, and decided to drop in and have a look around. I suppose I was curious about where that barefoot pilgrim was headed. I'd read the odd thing about the place years ago, but never actually been there. To be honest, I'm not entirely sure what I was expecting. Possibly just a regular English village, with an especially busy church.

The first thing that strikes you is the number of priests and vicars striding up and down the pavements. That and the fact that every other shop seems to be selling religious knick-knacks. Like those shops in seaside resorts that stock nothing but sticks of rock and buckets and spades and postcards. Whereas in these shops everything has a cross on it, or the face of Jesus. Or, more specifically, Our Lady of Walsingham.

It was only when I came across a noticeboard with a street map on it that I appreciated how many different denominations have set up their own little outposts there. Although as far as I could tell they all seem to rub along perfectly well.

Religious places make me slightly uneasy. Partly, I suspect, because of the intrinsic mysticism. But I do always rather worry that some spiritual hand might reach out and grab me. I'm sure I can't be alone in that. And Walsingham itself has about it the feel of a village from some 1950s black-and-white movie where the protagonist gradually discovers that there's no way out.

So, all in all, I was a little on edge as I made a quick tour of the place. I popped my head into the main shrine and managed to convince myself, despite it all being quite High Church and there being plenty of candles, etc., that the architecture was a little too modern for my taste. And that I like my religious buildings to have been around for a good four or five hundred years. There were quite a few people arriving, and it looked as if they were gearing themselves up for some sort of service, so I left them to it and bought a ticket to the museum up the road, and read all about the woman in the eleventh century and her visions and how people started to flock to the place, including Henry VIII – presumably, a few years before he had a change of heart and decided to raze the place to the ground.

I suspect I was rather hoping to bump into my barefoot pilgrim. At least then I'd have been able to ask him what he wanted from his visit – what his story was. But all the people I passed looked very well-shod, and there was no one obviously halt or lame. And I was beginning to feel a little disappointed when a fine drizzle began to settle over the village. I was about twenty yards from the Russian Orthodox chapel, so I slipped in there for a minute or two.

The chapel itself is nothing but a small plain room in what was once the railway station. Windowless, but lit by dozens of candles. And almost immediately I felt quite at home there – or as close to it as I've got these past few months. Around the walls were Eastern icons, with all their gold leaf and luminous blues and greens. And perhaps in the end that's all you need – the dark, the warmth. The candlelight, and the smell of hot wax. And some focus, such as an altar. Or the odd icon or two, to catch the light.

As I sat there, I began to appreciate how I was having a little moment of stillness, and I remember vaguely wondering if there were going to be tears. They seemed like the right sort of conditions. I can't say I would have minded. A good old cry, as I'm sure I've already noted, will sometimes do me the power of good. But it seemed there weren't. It was just a little peace that I was having. A little meditation. Some sense of stillness. And calm.

I've no idea how long I sat there. Ten minutes? Maybe more. And perhaps the fact that when I finally emerged from the chapel I was feeling a little light-headed contributed to the weirdness which followed. I was just standing around, stretching my legs. But as I stood there, with my mind still filled with candlelight, I thought I saw something in the distance – something in the drizzle, down the way.

If there had been singing, or prayers, or chanting I might have understood a little sooner. But all I heard were the muffled sound of footfalls – the sound of movement – as a band of thirty or forty souls slowly headed towards me.

As they grew nearer I felt the weight of their silence. There was nothing but their relentless collective shuffle. And even the children who walked along, holding the hands of their mothers and fathers, were solemnly mute. The silence hung over the whole party like a shroud.

And now I could see how one of the men carried in his arms a statue of Mary, clamped to his chest and tilted slightly, as if it was something he'd just picked up along the way. And someone else held a staff, with a brass cross at the tip. Their progress was made even stranger by the fact that nobody looked to left or right. They all kept their eyes fixed most concertedly on the road ahead. So that as they passed I had the sense that I had been quietly annihilated. Or that I was but a ghost to them.

All except for one – a little toddler, of about eighteen months or so, who was being carried in his mother's arms. He had his own eerie calm about him. And I couldn't help but notice how he held his hands in that same strange way – as if in mid-genuflection – as the apostles in the church in Salthouse. And just as Jesus does in all the statues of Mary and child.

As the group crept quietly by the child saw me and stared straight at me. He even turned in his mother's arms to keep his eyes on me. I'll be honest, the little fellow quite frightened the life out of me. I was convinced that, any minute, his little lips would part, he'd point a pudgy little finger at me and cry out, 'Adulterer' ... or ... 'Degenerate'.

Anyway, the silent throng carried on their way and

finally disappeared around the corner. I stood in the road, quite stunned. I have to say I didn't hang about much after that. I was in my car and out of there in next to no time. And the moment I got back to the village I went straight round to the Nelson and had a half of Woodforde's Wherry, chased down with a large brandy, just to settle my nerves.

I'm like a bloody sentry, obsessively patrolling my own little stretch of coastline – sometimes out there marching up and down the marshes three or four times a day. There's a little hut or hide out near Stiffkey where I'll often stop and eat an apple or a piece of flapjack. Especially when it's wet. If it's dry there's a hollow in the long grass that I'm particularly fond of, set back from the path. I've tucked myself away in there several times now, with nothing but the occasional birder puttering by, perfectly oblivious. Spying on twitchers has, I feel, a pleasing irony to it. Though so far I've witnessed nothing more incriminating than the odd adjustment of underwear.

I'm a bit of a late convert to the joys of walking. Of course, I've always been as willing as the next person to hike up some hill to admire the view. And I can see that there's something to be said for wandering through the woods in autumn and kicking up the leaves. But the sort of walking I do these days is more forced march than ramble. It never fails to get the blood moving round my body which must, I imagine, be of some benefit. But it's the way it gently shakes me up that I'm beginning to appreciate might have some positive influence on me.

Which is not to say I'm feeling healed, by any means. And yet there's definitely something in the simple mechanical action of sustained walking that seems to encourage my mind to quieten down a little. Like those parents who endlessly push a buggy round the block to get their babies off to sleep.

One of my self-appointed duties, aside from keeping an eye out for any belated Anglo-Saxon invaders, is to measure any additional minutes of daylight and gauge whether the sun gains any strength. Well, the days do indeed seem to be getting longer, albeit incrementally, but they also seem to be growing colder. I keep the fire going in my tiny cottage pretty much round the clock, which is only a problem in that I seem to be forever dragging bags of coal around the place.

I do wonder what the original pilgrims got out of their walking – the ones who hiked for days or even weeks to reach their destination. I mean, were their journeys carried out in an atmosphere of celebration or penance? The latter, I would imagine. We northern Europeans don't really go in for fervour. We'd rather focus on the guilt.

But we do like a bit of a procession. According to the little booklet I picked up at Walsingham museum, the band of silent pilgrims I recently encountered would have just hiked the mile or so up from the Slipper Chapel, where traditionally they would've removed their shoes in order to walk barefoot into town. But what were the early pilgrims after, exactly? Absolution? Or simply the desire to arrive, suitably exhausted, at what they considered to be a holy site?

I have to say, I find the whole idea of paying one's

respects to some saint's withered finger or shin-bone fairly gruesome. In fact, I'm pretty sure I once saw a photograph of a saint's head sitting pickled in a church somewhere. It really is quite barbaric. And yet I can see how people would be drawn to the idea of a relic. How could a sliver of the True Cross or a drop or two of Mary's own milk possibly fail to have some magic to it? And there are times in all our lives when we're in need of a bit of that.

It's not quite the same, I know, but a friend of mine happened to be living in Berlin when the Wall came down. I remember speaking to her on the phone as it was all going on. A week or two later a package landed on my doormat and in it was a small cardboard box with a note attached, explaining that it contained a tiny fragment of the Berlin Wall.

For all I know she just went out into her backyard and took a sledgehammer to a couple of breezeblocks and distributed the various bits to all her friends. But there's no doubt that in the days that followed, whenever we had people round and I happened to mention it to them, they all got mightily animated, and wanted to see it and hold it in their hand. As if it carried in it some charge, or potency. Some sense of its own history.

My first thought was that I was being mugged, or at best accosted. As I've already noted, I'm still quite highly strung when I'm out and about. And I suspect that as I shuffled down the High Street in Holt this afternoon I was miles away, lost in my own grey world, turning over some dismal thought or other, when I became increasingly conscious of someone creeping towards me, and threatening to impose themselves into my little bubble of misery. And a young person at that – which pretty much guarantees a mugging – someone who came scuttling up to me and grabbed me by the arm.

Well, 'grabbed' may be overstating it somewhat. But physical contact was definitely made. And being handled by strangers has always put my back up. So I must have recoiled. Then the anonymous youth was saying, 'Excuse me,' and apologising, as he could clearly see that he'd scared me half to death.

To be fair, the whole thing could have been resolved a good deal sooner if only his pronunciation hadn't been so poor. So that when he said 'Holbein' it had rhymed with 'Woodbine', as it is meant to, rather than 'runner bean' which was the way that it came out.

'Your Holbein book,' he said. 'I think I found it.'

And now I recognised him as the young man who'd

been behind the counter at the second-hand bookshop on my second visit. The one I'd rather unkindly likened to Kafka or Dostoevsky, and who, to my shame, turns out to be a very considerate individual. And when, at last, I'd worked out who he was and begun to grasp what it was he was talking about, he was already explaining how he'd mentioned the fact that I was looking for the book to Carol – who is most likely the woman I know as Jenny – and how it turned out that she'd had a look at it herself, after seeing me poring over it, and left it behind the counter.

'I've been keeping an eye out for you,' he told me, as he led me across the road to the shop, which, in itself, is just about enough to get any widow welling up. The idea, in fact, that anyone at all might be keeping an eye out for you.

Well, I'm assuming he must have been able to see that I was in a bit of a state because when we reached the shop he even offered to make me a cup of tea. But I declined – paid for the book, thanked him and got back out of there as quickly as possible. Primarily out of embarrassment, but also because now that I finally had the book in my hands again and what with him being so kind to me I didn't want to burst into tears right there in the shop.

I got as far as the car park before stopping and flipping through the book's pages. It really is an unexceptional edition. And one, apparently, which used to reside on the shelves of the library of Norwich Art College. All four corners are bent and battered. Oh, those rough and scruffy undergraduates! The plain brown cover is partially bleached from sunlight. But the actual plates are close to perfect. And the paintings themselves are . . . well, they're simply exquisite.

I waited till I got back home before having a proper look at it. I pushed the boat out and put the kettle on. And since I'm in a mood of contrition, I feel I owe a word or two's apology to the two gentlemen in *The Ambassadors*. The chap on the left does indeed look rather bulky, but that's probably as much to do with all the furs and so forth slung around him as his actual girth. The chap on the right also has a powerful presence, but this is mainly due to the decidedly jazzy design of his dressing gown.

The woman with the bonnet is not quite as inundated as I'd imagined. A single thrush stands to attention over one shoulder and there's the odd sprig of greenery here and there. But close scrutiny reveals that the squirrel in her lap actually has a tiny chain around its neck, so it's not as if the creature had been magnetically drawn towards her from the wilderness.

But the revelation is *Christina of Denmark*. The weird thing is that I'm actually familiar with this painting. I've stood before it on several occasions, but never properly appreciated what a wonderful piece of work it is. The girl's white face peers out from the top of a heap of deep black velvet. Her hands, neatly crossed over a pair of cream gloves, are the only other source of light. But it's her steady gaze which holds you. Once she's caught your eye there's no letting go.

I'd flipped through the whole book and come back to her two or three times before I checked the text for any info. And it was only then that I learnt that she was dressed in black as she was in mourning – that she was a young widow – and that Holbein had been shipped out to Brussels to paint her as yet another prospective bride for Henry VIII.

Well, aside from the fact that the poor little thing looks barely old enough to have seen off a first husband, let alone be contemplating the perils of having big, bad Henry as her second, the beautiful creature is a widow! And so I'm bound to wonder if that's the reason I've been so desperate to get my hands on the book. I mean, when I picked it up last week did I unconsciously register her mourning clothes? I don't believe so. I don't think it ever crossed my mind.

And then suddenly I'm crying. A proper little outburst, the kind which I've not had in quite a while. The poor sweet thing. Married at the age of eleven. Widowed at the age of thirteen. And still only sixteen, by my calculations, when Holbein came a-calling, on the orders of Henry VIII.

In fact, she was widowed a second time by the age of twenty-three. To be honest, I'm not quite sure why I should be getting myself so upset about a girl who lived the best part of five hundred years ago. Not least because, according to the book, she had a good forty-five years of independence, as the Regent of Lorraine. Whatever that entailed. I suppose it's the idea of her being married off at such a tender age, and to such old duffers. And having to drag all that black velvet around behind her and play at being the widow for so many years. That really does upset me. Although I can't help but feel that my pity for her is somehow wrapped up in some sort of pity for myself.

Anyway, once I got a grip and made myself a cup of coffee, and had another skim through my precious book, I began to appreciate that it's not just the eyes of my poor child-widow that move me. Despite all the props and pomp and finery – and Holbein's undoubted genius – it's the eyes of all his subjects that draw you in. They're all so sad. And so solemn. All except for dear Christina. Who is simply serene.

I am, there's no use me denying it, an inveterate list-maker. So perhaps I should retract that earlier criticism regarding my husband, and men in general, for all their newspaper-reading, since what is the writing of lists if not a deluded attempt to create some sense of order in one's own small corner of the universe?

I always tend to think it's a relatively recent development. Something I've only picked up in the last year or two. Then I'll bump into someone I've not seen in ages and they'll catch me at it and say, God, are you still making those endless bloody lists of yours? Which always comes as rather a shock to me.

My ideal template is a plain sheet of A4, folded in the middle, to create a two-ply rectangle, approximately eight inches by six. Whatever I scratch and scrawl within its borders is the business of that particular day of my life made flesh.

Domestic chores, such as banking, shopping, etc., are entered in the top left quarter. Less pressing but possibly more important matters, such as letters, phone calls, etc., occupy the middle ground. In all that clean white space on the right-hand side I mark down any specific appointments, for example: '2 p.m. – Dentist', with the 2 p.m. underlined and circled, so that I can't miss it.

I might also note down this half of the page any radio programmes which sound potentially interesting. Or a piece of music I've heard somewhere and am considering buying. Or even some odd little idea I've made a note of, that I plan to follow up.

The bottom third of the page is where all the heavy matter sinks to, such as anything to do with the Inland Revenue or entreaties to visit some aged aunt in Aldershot – commitments which, having not been met on the Monday, will reappear on Tuesday's list. And, most likely, Wednesday's too. But written quickly, so as to avoid the thought that one might never actually get around to them. And on busy days these lower reaches might even be cordoned off from the rest of the list by a thick black line, from one edge of the paper to the other, to prevent them contaminating the items above. Because, just as list-writing can be a means of ensuring that every last thing is remembered, it can also be a highly effective method of procrastination – essentially nothing but a list of good intentions which, once written down, need not be dwelt upon for another day.

Anyway, I mention my lists here because, over these last few months, they have been noticeable only by their absence. I suppose if you're not particularly engaged in the present tense and having trouble projecting yourself into the future, there's not an awful lot to be writing down. And if you really do need to remind yourself to, say, put the bins out on the Tuesday, you can just write it in your diary. Which is just a list spread over time.

The moment John died my list-making ground to a halt. And when, a few days later, I had a peek at the last list I'd made, just out of curiosity, its contents seemed so utterly trivial I wondered how I could ever have lived a life where such things held any sway.

Because by then the only list in town would've been ...

GET DEATH CERTIFICATE

VISIT SOLICITOR

MEDICATION?

I entered, I suppose, a life no longer containable by a folded sheet of A4. Or, rather, a life in which the hope of getting on top of things was abandoned. And, of course, in truth I've never succeeded in scratching out every single entry on any list I've ever written. If I had I would've simply created a vacuum which would've demanded the creation of a new list of other, even more exacting tasks.

But in the last couple of days I've actually written a new list or two. Tentative little things, embarrassingly modest when compared to those titanic, all-encompassing lists of yesteryear. But encouraging, just the same. Scrawled on the back of a flyer for the Wells and Walsingham Light Railway and seal trip timetables. The young shoots of future planning. The bright new hope of lists to come.

Talking of saints, I've always had a sneaking respect for Simeon Stylites, the original pillar saint who spent half his life perched on top of said pillar, delivering sermons, dispensing wisdom and subsisting on nothing but whatever snacks the general public felt inclined to toss up to him.

It's a pretty extreme way of showing one's devotion. Like those chaps in India who sit with one arm raised above their head for year upon year, until the fingernails curl into coils and the whole limb goes as black as a prune.

As for pillar-living, setting aside the obvious concerns, re sleeping and bathroom arrangements, I do rather balk at such a public display of devotion. I suppose pillar saint-dom is always going to attract the more extrovert type. Whereas, if I ever went down the ascetic route – and, let's be honest, if I were to make a name for myself in that department I'd have to be getting on with it pretty damned quick – I'd be more inclined to seek out some little cell or cave and go about it quite quietly. I wouldn't say no to the odd bar of chocolate, but I really couldn't be doing with great hordes of people. How would one find the time to reflect?

Well, there's not much point my pretending that I just tripped over the Slipper Chapel this morning, as if I just happened to be wending my way around those tiny lanes out there. The fact is I'd picked up a couple of leaflets when I was over in Walsingham, one of which had a little calendar of events tucked inside. And I've always been rather intrigued by the idea of the Stations of the Cross. But, for what it's worth, I went along more as an observer than a potential participant.

I'd had an extra glass or two of wine last night, which didn't help matters. When I woke I felt about as bad as I've felt all week, and it seemed to take me an extra hour just to get myself up and moving. In fact, I was pretty sure I was going to be late. But either I'd got the times wrong or what I'd taken to be the start of the service was actually when people were just meeting up. So I'd gone haring down the little lanes, not entirely sure where I was going, then suddenly, out in the middle of nowhere, there was this massive car park, with rows of coaches and hundreds of people milling about.

I parked up and, albeit a little self-consciously, joined the general stream of people. We wound around a couple of buildings and came out into a large open area, with an oval patch of grass in the middle, and maybe 150 chairs arranged across it.

I feel obliged to note that it was exceptionally cold this morning – if only to explain how odd it was to see a lectern and microphone set up at the front, on a low dais. But I suppose if you're going to do the Stations of the Cross this time of year and you've got a fair-sized crowd of people you want to be sure everyone can hear what's going on.

I walked down one side, past a series of wooden crosses, each about six foot tall, around which, I assumed, the Stations would be taking place. Not for the first time, it occurred to me what remarkable power is contained in a simple wooden cross. You just take two lengths of wood and nail them together and, for anyone brought up in a Christian society, it fairly stops you in your tracks.

Anyway, by now I was simply hanging around, with little or no idea what was going to happen but not wanting to ask anyone for fear of drawing attention to myself. So I just did my best to look deeply earnest, and whenever anyone caught my eye I did that dreadful apologetic smile/grimace I tend to do at parties when I don't know anyone.

At the far end of the open space a small crowd was buzzing around a trestle table. I mean, really quite frenetic, like the crush around a WI stall when the cakes first come out. So I drifted over in that general direction and, when I was close enough, went up on my tiptoes to try to see what all the fuss was about.

A wooden box sat in the middle of the table – about the same size as a small harmonium, with a slot in the top. And all around the table people were bent over small squares of paper, scribbling little messages. I came around one side and saw a sign beside the box which said, simply, 'PETITIONS'. Some of the people scrawling away were using their spare hand to shield what they were writing. Then folding them up, and posting them into the wooden box.

Over the years, my exposure to the Catholic Church has been pretty minimal, so it took me a moment or two to work out what people might be petitioning *for* exactly. Namely, help. Help with their bad leg. Or their sick mother. And, one imagines, in many cases, for help with their own troubled mind. Seeing the rate at which those little notes were being folded up and posted I was suddenly struck by the colossal weight of pain and anguish all around me, and was profoundly moved by it. And not just the idea of it existing in that particular churchyard, but right across the land. That, at any given moment, despite appearances to the contrary, half the people you pass in the street are suffering their own private torment, and just doing their best to get from one minute to the next.

Anyway, it seemed a little indecent of me to stand there watching these people writing their private little messages, so I wandered off. I wonder what actually happens to all those bits of paper. At some point, presumably, the wooden box is carted off to a secret location, where a priest picks out each petition and blesses them . . . or reads them aloud. To be honest, I haven't a clue what the process might consist of. In other cultures they'd quite possibly set fire to them, as an act of cleansing, or conveying the contents to the appropriate place. Perhaps they burn them here, once they've been read, or dealt with. Not for any mystical reasons, but just for the sake of privacy. I mean, what else are you going to do with them?

There was still no sense of the service starting, so I carried on round the corner and found myself in a tiny courtyard, where an old stone font stood and a steady trickle of water poured from the pipes in all four corners into the trough below. Around each one, people were politely queuing, clutching plastic bottles, many of which were identical and I assume had been bought somewhere on the premises. But some people had their own bottles, which they'd brought along themselves.

Everyone was doing their best to be patient, but you could see that here and there people were getting a little browned off, not least those waiting behind one chap who was filling the sort of vessel you'd expect to see at the taps on a campsite. Of course, nobody actually said anything to him. But you could tell that people were thinking, 'What's he planning to do – take a ruddy bath in it?'

I went and stood over by a wall, so as not to get in the way. And I suppose because I was just standing there watching, rather than queuing, I must have stuck out like a sore thumb. After a minute or two I became aware of an older woman, in her seventies or eighties, giving me the once-over. I turned and unleashed in her direction a smile of maximum inanity. She nodded back at me, but kept on staring, until I felt obliged to explain myself.

'I'm just an observer,' I said. Which was perfectly true, but sounded faintly ridiculous, as if I was there on behalf of the United Nations or some other international organisation.

She gave me a little smile. Then nodded towards the far end of the font. 'I'm waiting for my sister,' she said. I looked over and saw the woman to whom she was referring, hanging around behind the chap with the five-gallon drum.

'If he's not careful,' she said, 'they're going to suddenly turn and set upon him.'

We both stood and watched for another couple of moments. Then, if only for something to say as much as anything else, I asked her what people actually did with the water.

'I mean, do you drink it?' I said.

She turned and had a good, long look at me now, presumably having worked out that I was (a) most certainly not a Catholic, and (b) quite possibly the biggest idiot she'd ever come across.

'No, no,' she said. 'It's just to have around the house. You know, in case a priest happens to drop by.'

It was the sort of answer which gives with one hand and takes with the other. But as we'd at least established that, like certain medicine, it wasn't to be taken internally, I assumed that the priest would use it for some sort of blessing or anointment. So I smiled and nodded very slowly, as if some great truth had been revealed to me.

I didn't want her to think me rude, or feel that her efforts had been wasted. I also wanted to bring this whole embarrassing conversation to a close. So I said goodbye and headed off, as if I had urgent business elsewhere. Then, as soon as I was out of sight, I slowed down again. By now the place was getting very busy. There was a huge shop – in fact, pretty much a mini-market – which I might have been tempted to have a look around if I could've only found the entrance. But I appeared to be round the back of it, peering in through a smallish window. And, even at the time, it occurred to me that this was quite a reasonable representation of how I felt wandering around among all these pilgrims.

My only other distraction before the main event was when I spent a couple of minutes queuing up to visit a tiny chapel. I quite fancied immersing myself in a little more quiet candlelight. But as the queue slowly shuffled forward it slowly dawned on me that there was not going to be a great deal of solitude in there. And I've never been that keen on being in confined spaces with lots of other people. My nerve finally cracked about three yards from the chapel entrance. A priest was standing by the doorway, like a bouncer. He seemed to be eyeing up each individual as they passed – a sort of spiritual frisking. And as I was just about the only person queuing who wasn't carrying an unlit candle it was pretty clear that I was an interloper. Even if I'd happened to locate the special stall where they sold the candles, I wouldn't have known what to do with it when I got in there – would, no doubt, have curtsied at quite the wrong moment, or put the lit candle in the wrong place, or set fire to something/someone.

Besides, I had the sneaking suspicion that, deep in his ear, the priest had a tiny receiver, through which information was currently being transmitted regarding a woman of stupendous ignorance in all things Catholic, especially holy water, who was starting to get on everyone's nerves. So at the very last moment I bolted, as I rather seem to have got into the habit of doing lately. And spent the next few minutes doing a little more wandering. Until, at last, I heard the screech of feedback over the Tannoy, as a microphone was tested, and everyone started heading towards the open space.

I walked back around the perimeter and tucked myself away by the wall closest to the car park, so that if I found the whole thing too weird or overwhelming, or happened to find myself being chased by an angry mob, I might have half a chance of making it to my car and getting away.

I suppose I'm not used to being around religious people – at least, not in such numbers. Among my friends I would estimate that there are, at most, two or three firm believers, the rest subscribing to something which hovers between agnosticism and atheism. By which I mean they don't subscribe to anything much at all. In all likelihood, they said their prayers and sang hymns every day at school assembly and nowadays troop into church for weddings and christenings and funerals maybe once or twice a year. They might have some sense of something significant off in the shadows. Something which is only ever really called upon in times of adversity, at which point its lack of substance and all-round inchoate nature is rather alarmingly laid bare.

As I glanced around me at my co-congregants this morning I couldn't help but try to identify some common characteristic. If not quite the saintly gold-leaf aura, then at least some sense of spiritual self-confidence. Of course, I was working on the basis that everyone else present was both a) a believer . . . and b) that their belief was topped right up to the brim. But that is to assume that faith is by definition a solid thing – unshakeable . . . constant. Whereas, there's every reason that it might wax and wane. If so, is a pilgrimage also a way of recharging one's spiritual battery? I imagine it probably is.

The last of the stragglers were taking their seats now and trying to find a space around the perimeter wall and I was beginning to get a little nervy. This was, after all, the lights-going-down part of the performance, prior to the conductor striding out towards the podium and tapping his baton on the music stand. I was worried about my not knowing when to bow or close my eyes or when to speak – or indeed what I was meant to say when I did. Not simply because I wanted to avoid making an even greater fool of myself than I'd already succeeded in doing, but because I genuinely didn't want to disrupt the proceedings. I felt quite strongly that I was a guest – albeit an uninvited one – at someone else's ceremony and the best way for me to show some respect for what was going on was to be as inconspicuous as possible.

All I knew about the Stations of the Cross was that it basically consists of a circuit, and that the congregation's focus slowly shifts from one designated site to another, which this morning was marked out by the wooden crosses, rather than the tableaux that you get inside a church. The priest at the microphone appeared to have overall authority, but just as things were about to get started two or three other priests appeared, one of whom had a staff with a cross at its tip and another had a candle the size of an artillery shell.

Everyone grew quiet. And I suddenly saw how I was part of a great gathering of people outdoors on a freezing winter's day, and in such stillness now that the only sound was the cackle of crows in some neighbouring field, and the wind high up in the cold, bare trees.

Then the fellow at the lectern began his incantation, and everyone turned to face the appropriate cross.

Those first words echoed around the stone walls of the surrounding buildings. The actual phrases might have been somewhat foreign, but the language and the manner in which they were delivered were quite familiar. And when the priest paused and the whole congregation began to utter their part in unison I suddenly felt very much at home.

It was the same haunting murmur, barely rising or falling from a monotone, with which I'd recited the Lord's Prayer right through my childhood. The same shared taking-of-a-breath. What I had identified, in fact, was the tribal chant of the British Christian. And hearing it again – feeling it now resonate all around me – very nearly reduced me to tears.

The three priests, with their staff and candle, moved on. And at each cross a few words were delivered from the lectern. Most of the congregation bowed their heads, but I noticed one or two individuals, including a man in his seventies, who insisted on going down on one knee. Then there was a little more call and response between the priest and the congregation. And, minute by minute, the focus slowly swung around the garden's perimeter, like the invisible hand of a clock, with the story of the Passion echoing over the Tannoy system, and nothing but the rattling trees filling the space in between.

By the time the priests had moved on to the third or fourth Station I noticed a little girl over to my right. She was about five years old, all wrapped up in a thick little coat, with a matching scarf and hat. She'd found herself a twig and was using it to dig out the dirt between the flagstones – was happily chatting away to herself, and scratching and digging out the moss and dirt with considerable industry.

I remember being about her age, or possibly even a little older, and tugging up the long, rough grass at the bottom of the garden, and washing it in an enamel bowl. With real water that I'd insisted my mother pour out for me. Then tying it up on the wire fence for the sun to dry it. God knows what I thought I was up to. But I remember taking the whole enterprise very seriously. At lunchtimes in the summer holidays I used to inform my mother what I'd been up to that morning and how busy an afternoon I had before me, as if playing was a job of work.

The hand of the clock continued to slowly sweep around the crosses. And all the while that little girl kept digging between the flagstones, lost in her own little ritual. She appeared not to be paying any attention. But I couldn't help but think that some of the talk of blood and sin and crucifixion was bound to seep into some corner of her mind. And that, if nothing else, some day, fifty or sixty years hence, she might attend a church service of some sort and hear a phrase or simply the collective murmur of all those voices and it would stir up some feelings deep within her. Something to do with family and childhood, and even faith.

I'm not entirely sure what I was hoping for over at the Slipper Chapel. If not necessarily the whole falling-away-of-scales-from-the-eyes routine then some glimmer . . . of something or other. Some sense of wheels beginning to turn.

If nothing else, it made me appreciate that I do rather envy the believers. I envy them their rituals and all the accompanying paraphernalia – their candles and rosaries and incense and all that bowing and genuflecting. And not least the coming together, in the actual service. In something ancient – or at least apparently ancient. Something bigger than oneself. Devotion really is a form of surrender, perhaps even self-abnegation. And over the last few months there has been many a time when I would have heartily welcomed the opportunity to escape myself, if only for a minute or two.

Whatever I was after, I'm almost certain that I didn't quite find it. I could, I suppose, have fallen to my knees and asked for salvation, but deep down I would've felt like such a hypocrite. I suspect it was the idea of the Stations that particularly drew me to it. I don't want to sound like some old crank but any ritual which incorporates a circle or a circuit must have at least half a chance of generating some sort of energy. I'm sure even the lowliest physicist would back me up on that.

I'm just a little frustrated that whenever I consider such things these days I seem to be doing so through the eyes of an anthropologist. I observe. I might even appreciate. But I can't quite seem to lose myself.

Anyway, it's fair to say that I arrived back home a tad disappointed. I bought the paper and boiled myself an egg. And as I sat there, carefully lopping off the top of the egg, I thought, 'How about this for an austere little ritual.' With the salt and pepper waiting to be cast about the place and all the soldiers lined up in a neat little row.

They had some psychiatric academic on the radio this morning, banging on about something to do with 'The Unconscious'. I managed to keep up with him for about five minutes before he completely lost me and I had to turn it off. To be perfectly honest, the whole thing was starting to freak me out.

I've always acknowledged that there exists somewhere within me something commonly referred to as The Unconscious, or an unconscious mind. I've always talked as if I accept that it is there. But I think perhaps I must have imagined some set-up whereby when I'm awake it's almost totally dormant. Like a lake, with all manner of ugly stuff brimming about in the cold, dark depths which thankfully only reveals itself when I'm asleep.

But over the last few months I've had to reassess this little model and, specifically, how, in certain circumstances, that part of the mind usually kept packed away in the bottom drawer can suddenly spring out and threaten to overwhelm everything else. A week or two after John's death I caught myself staring at the cover of a newspaper. I realised that I couldn't make any sense of it – not even the headlines. For a second I thought it might be the onset of one of my migraine/blind-spot episodes. But it wasn't. I was looking . . . and I'm pretty sure I was seeing. But there was no comprehension to speak of at all. My own interpretation is that it was just that my mind had become utterly flooded with the stuff that's usually kept well out of the way. As if the reservoir of my unconscious had risen to such a level that it had seeped into the rest of my mind.

When I was at school I shared a room with a lovely girl called Sidney, though I'm sure that can't have been her real name. She was a rather timid little thing – terribly earnest and quite determined that she was one day going to be a Famous Mathematician. Little Sidney's problem was that she used to sleepwalk. I'd wake in the middle of the night and hear her pottering about the place. The first time she did it I thought she was just getting up to go to the loo, but after a couple of minutes I realised she was still footling around, so I turned the light on and found her on the floor, rooting about under the bed.

She was always at it – wandering up and down and banging into things. Or scratching at the walls, like some restless soul. Sometimes she'd chatter away to herself while she was in mid-sleepwalk. I once woke to find her standing at the window with the curtains wide open, nattering away like a gibbon. Which was pretty creepy, let me tell you. And, since I used to find the whole thing rather fascinating, on this particular occasion I slipped out of bed and tiptoed over to her side. I'd learnt that whenever she went off on one of her little walkabouts it was best just to try and gently steer her back to her bed, without waking her. But this one time I crept over and I began to talk to her – these quite innocent little enquiries. To try and get her to tell me what was going on.

It sounds almost cruel, but it really was nothing but honest-to-goodness curiosity. It was as if some secret hatch had been left open. I felt like a psychic, talking to someone on the other side.

I can't remember now what it was she was ranting on about. I sometimes wonder what became of the poor little mite. I half expect to see her picture in the paper, next to a story about her being awarded the Nobel Prize for Maths. It really wouldn't surprise me. But I'll never forget that sense of her wandering through the caves and caverns of her own unconscious and me briefly having this string-and-tin-can telephone, through which I imagined she could report back to me.

God only knows the state of my own unconscious mind these days – what chasms of angst and swamps of melancholia are bubbling away down there. It must look like the bloody Somme. Or Nagasaki. And who knows if such a ravaged landscape ever really recovers. If I've grasped anything over the last few months it's that grief . . . or mourning . . . or whatever you want to call it, is not a continuum. Is not an arrow on a successful company's sales chart, rising inexorably towards the north-east. You don't wake up each morning feeling a tiny bit better than the day before.

I fully anticipate that five years from now – or ten, or twenty, if I manage to last that long – I shall be shuffling through my garden, with a trug in one hand and a copy of *Woman's Weekly* in the other and, for no discernible reason, I will be struck again by the magnitude of John's death. And it will rip right through me and rend me asunder with just as much force as the day I first heard about it, three months ago.

Right up until the day I jumped into my car and shot up here John was still receiving a fair bit of post and even the odd phone call, as if he still moved among us. As if someone was trying to test my resolve.

It's mostly junk mail, of course. Or some flunky on the phone from some far-flung call centre who remains unmoved in the face of my protestations, convinced that I'm just trying to throw him off the scent. No, *really*, I feel like saying. I was there, at the bloody funeral. That was me, right down at the front.

For the first few weeks I replied to every note, politely explaining the situation. But after a couple of months, having received yet another letter from some credit-card company fishing for business – and possibly even a company I'd already written to the previous month – I would just scrawl 'NO LONGER AT THIS ADDRESS. RETURN TO SENDER' across the front and march it straight round to the post box. And on one occasion, when I was feeling particularly tetchy, 'THIS MAN IS DEAD'.

Since John's death/demise/unexplained disappearance I've received three batches of post from his old company. The first arrived in a large brown envelope, with a covering letter explaining that everything addressed to him was being dealt with by the post room, unless it clearly had nothing to do with the business, in which case it would be forwarded to me. It's odd, but the arrival of that first small stack of letters provoked in me a sort of prurient excitement. What was I hoping for exactly? Some sickeningly explicit piece of pornography? Some note from a woman at the Edinburgh office who'd sunk one too many margaritas at some annual shindig and let John put his hand up her skirt?

The actual contents couldn't have been less racy – mostly invitations to industry junkets at various golf/racecourses. Or offers of discount gym membership. But in the second package there was one letter, handwritten, with the word 'PERSONAL' in the top left-hand corner. That's what first aroused my suspicions – along with the fact that the stamps were Swedish. I wasn't aware that either one of us actually knew any Swedes. And as I opened it up I felt that same strange giddiness stir in me again.

It was handwritten. The signature was barely legible, so I flipped the letter over and just started skimming through the text. There was certainly no shortage of affection in its two or three pages. But it became pretty clear pretty quickly that there had been no hanky-panky. And, soon, that it was in fact from some Swedish chap, rather than some pneumatic blonde Swede-ess. Still, I didn't give up hope. Who knows? Maybe John and this Swedish chappie had been up to no good whilst in each other's company. Perhaps there had been a night out and a late-night taxi into Soho. Or even just some shared confidences, which were currently outside of my realm. Again, I was disappointed. Some reference was made to a couple of drinks following a previous meeting. But Sven, or Henning, or whatever he was called, was now just getting in touch to ask if John was planning to attend the meeting in Stockholm. To which, the short answer was, of course, No. He was not.

Very strange. It was as if I'd unwittingly developed an appetite for sordid revelation. Something that might knock John's saintly reputation down a peg or two. Either that or I just wanted to hear about something that might even things out a little. Or rub a little salt in the wound.

So, I suppose, in the end I got my just desserts, etc. If you keep on scratching away at something you're almost bound to make it bleed. At our solicitor's behest I'd spent a couple of hours in John's study, trawling through his papers and trying to unearth one or two elusive documents. Had worked my way down to the bottom drawer of one of the filing cabinets and right at the back discovered an old cigar box with a couple of elastic bands wrapped round it, to stop the contents spilling out.

It may just be that I had too much blood pumping round my head to properly grasp the situation. But inside there was a small clutch of letters, all folded and refolded as if they'd each been read a hundred times. And I'd opened up the first one and was sitting down on the floor and reading it before I'd even taken a breath.

The tone might have been decidedly casual, cool even,

but reading between the lines it was pretty obvious how serious she was. She was quoting bloody Goethe, for Christ's sake. And talking about her favourite movies. She was modestly presenting herself as the most sophisticated woman ever to walk the earth.

And I suddenly worked out who this woman was. Who'd loved my husband. I was halfway down the second page before I even recognised her handwriting – that tell-tale, overly elaborate copperplate. The pen had put such pressure on the paper that I'd practically engraved the thing.

It was the barely concealed desperation that finally did for me. How much I clearly wanted him. And suddenly it all came rushing back – the dread of what life might be like without him. Please God, I remember thinking in those few weeks between our first meeting and the brokering of some unspoken contract. Please God, don't let me lose this one. This one's good and kind and decent. This is the man for me.

I couldn't now say for certain how much time elapsed between me seeing Paul in Cambridge and my coming up to Norfolk to spend the weekend with him. A month, maybe. Perhaps a little longer. At the time, I'm sure, it must have felt like an eternity, and long enough for me to become convinced that Paul would lose interest and for the whole thing to wither on the vine.

As far as John was concerned I was simply visiting some old friend from college. Rather than spin some intricate web of lies involving a real person I conjured up an entirely fictitious individual. It just seemed a good deal easier and, in the event, John had less trouble with me hiking off to Norfolk for the weekend than Ginny, who'd perhaps paid a little more attention to our conversations over the previous couple of decades and was now finding it difficult to give credence to this dear old pal of mine who'd just popped up, completely out of the blue.

Anyway, on the Friday morning John pecked me on the cheek and went off to work. I remember standing in the kitchen and giving it serious consideration, but felt not the merest flicker of guilt. In fact, it took some restraint on my part not to jump in my car and plough straight into the rush hour. As I recall, I managed to wait until about half past nine before setting off, but I must've still got up here by mid-afternoon. Checked into the hotel, unpacked, made myself a cup of tea, and still had a good couple of hours to hang about.

It was Paul who recommended the hotel – a place which, even back then, was fairly grand. The village was probably somewhat scruffier and I doubt there were quite so many letting agents. But it was still a pretty little place. We'd arranged for Paul to join me straight after work on the Friday evening, which meant we'd have all of Saturday together and possibly some of Sunday, depending on whether he managed to swap shifts with a colleague ... or something along those lines.

It really doesn't seem that long ago. But, to put it into some sort of context, at the time mobile phones were still considered to be the toys almost exclusively of city traders. I mention this only because, having bathed and powdered myself and done my best to make myself irresistible in every conceivable way, I didn't dare leave the hotel to take a stroll out on the saltmarshes – the same saltmarshes on which I now seem to spend half my waking hours – in case Paul tried to call me via the hotel switchboard. So I just flitted about the room and sat and waited. Then flitted about the room some more.

It had been established a good couple of weeks earlier as being quite impractical for me to stay with Paul. The whole situation was *difficult*. Was *complicated*. And, in the vaguest way, something to do with the cottage being tied to the trust which employed Paul. As if my very presence would have provided sufficient grounds for the terms of the lease to be broken, or the neighbours to be scandalised. Or to set in motion some other inexplicable process, which would lead to Paul finding himself thrown out and wandering the lanes of Norfolk, destitute.

Of course, I now know this to be absolute claptrap. In my defence, all I'll say is that it didn't seem so at the time. It seemed a little odd, but not suspicious. Paul had sworn blind that there was no beautiful, dutiful wife squirrelled away back at the cottage. And he appeared to be just as frustrated by the situation as me. I simply thought to myself, 'What quaint, anachronistic codes of behaviour they have out in the shires.'

Paul finally pitched up around five-thirty. I stood and watched at the window as he pulled into the car park. I was desperate to run down to him, but didn't want to jump all over him in public – wanted to do that when we were alone. So I was obliged to spend another few minutes pacing my room. Then stood at the door, watching the lights above the lift, until it finally reached my floor. And the doors slowly crept open and I went belting down the corridor and threw my arms around him.

More than anything else, I just remember being so utterly, utterly relieved. I felt that I was myself again. Felt like I could breathe. For what it's worth, Paul seemed about as pleased to see me as I was to see him. And the rest of the evening proceeded in pretty much the way we'd both anticipated, the only surprise being that we both got quite seriously drunk.

After breakfast on the Saturday morning we had a stroll

around the village, then drove over to Holkham Sands, where we sat and looked out over that long, wide beach, with that endless sky above it for what seemed like the entire day. I'm not generally one for trying to quantify my little moments of happiness. What good does it do you in the end? But I doubt there have been many days in my life when I've come close to feeling half as hopeful as I did that afternoon.

I'd love to know what we talked about, wrapped up in the confines of Paul's jacket and each other's arms. I can't recall a single word. Though the words aren't particularly important. What's important is that sense of calm and warmth. And resolution. Most of which is as lost to me now as the conversation itself.

I was still high as a kite later that evening, back in my hotel room, when Paul told me, ever so quietly, how he'd split up from his partner earlier that year, whilst going to great pains to point out how this had all happened long before the two of us had met. Rather perversely, I took some reassurance from this news – from the fact that there *had* been someone. But that she was now well out of the way.

It was pretty clear that he was still quite cut up by the whole thing. Indeed, I remember comforting him. And when I look back now I find that scene particularly sickening. Possibly because my sympathy was so utterly disingenuous, and masked nothing but my own insecurities. And possibly because Paul was prepared to accept such consolation when, as it later transpired, the relationship whose demise we both purported to mourn was, in fact, far from dead.

I sometimes wonder what I was hoping for. How I thought things might ultimately turn out. That I would simply leave John and trot off to the sticks to be with Paul? A man who understood the weather . . . and appreciated the seasons . . . who could confidently identify the birds and plants and trees? And that the two of us would find our own untied, uncomplicated cottage, where we would raise chickens and grow our own potatoes? Well, frankly, yes. I think that was pretty much the long and short of it. And I'm still a little shocked at just how readily I would have abandoned John and my dearest friends for this relative stranger. Unless all I was looking for was an excuse to do precisely that.

On the Saturday night, as we sat at our table in the hotel restaurant, I remember Paul glancing around him in what I wrongly interpreted as a man impressed, or even intimidated, by his surroundings. It would be a couple of months before I put two and two together and realised that it was far more likely the fear of him seeing a member of staff or fellow-diner who had some connection to his own village. Someone who might convey to his ex-partner (who still happened to live just down the road from him) that he was out having dinner with another woman – and a much older woman at that.

But before I was able to review that scene in a new light, and even before we'd sat down to have that dinner, when I'd rather patronisingly thought that Paul had never eaten in a decent restaurant, I have one other treasured memory. We were lying in bed up in my room and Paul happened to pick up a book that I was reading. He must have found a passage that he liked the sound of and read a couple of lines from it out loud. I remember that I was lying next to him, with my eyes closed. He stopped. And I asked him to carry on. I remember the words taking shape in the room. That lovely, lovely voice. I felt . . . such safety. I could feel myself begin to drift away. Like a child, being read to by a parent. And, like a child slipping into sleep, you sometimes force yourself awake. Perhaps because you don't want to go to sleep just yet. Or because you're worried about the strange dreams that sleep might bring. Or simply because you're happy here, with that steady voice slowly falling all around you. And that you want to stay right here, forevermore.

Well, that was about as good as it got. On the Sunday morning Paul made a call to one of his colleagues – a conversation which was, apparently, inconclusive. And I was informed that he'd have to drive over to the reserve and see what was going on. After a moment's thought I announced, quite breezily, that I might as well hang about for a couple of extra hours and that he could ring me once it was clear what was happening. But Paul doubted that it would be worth it. I took a breath. Actually, I said, it would be quite conceivable for me to book another night at the hotel. I could easily come up with some excuse for John. Then Paul could pop back over in the evening. But before I'd even finished I could see that Paul was beginning to get irritated. And that the more I tried to accommodate him the more irritated he became.

I hadn't a clue what was going on. I could feel myself floundering. But what so upset me was the cold, clear realisation that I wanted Paul more than he wanted me. In any relationship one or the other of you is always in the driving seat. Over time, that power may grow, or diminish. It might even shift from one party to the other. But at any point both people know, deep down, who has the upper hand. Who can walk away and not get hurt. And if you're somehow convinced that you're in the one relationship which exists on a plane above and beyond such selfish forces – a relationship which is poised in perfect and permanent equilibrium, then all I can say is you're fooling nobody but yourself.

On that Sunday morning I was suddenly confronted with the fact that it was me doing all the clinging. And Paul withdrawing. Paul applying the brakes. You'd think I might have had some idea which way the wind was blowing. But when you fall that badly for someone it's probably because of something you need rather than something they have to offer. I wonder how long it took me to work that out? All I know is that, at the time, it was as if the ground had just opened up beneath me. We said our goodbyes and had a little hug. And I think I just about managed to hold it all together until he was out of sight. Then I rather fell apart. In fact, it would be no exaggeration to say that I felt that my whole world was at an end.

I've still not got much of an appetite, or inclination to cook myself a proper meal. I should probably make more of an effort. I should eat my greens. I should eat more beans and lentils. Should give up the fags, and keep my weekly intake of booze down to whatever is currently governmentally acceptable. I should drink less coffee and drink more water. A lot more water. Should positively drown myself in the stuff. I should do more exercise. I should learn to love myself. And every morning I should bow down to the sun. But, generally speaking, I find I really can't be bothered. I'm newly widowed, for Chrissake. Give me a fucking break.

As I've already noted, this time of year I get a little obsessive about the extra minutes of daylight. You do sometimes sense darkness's grip beginning to slip. But it's never quite fast enough.

I've always been of the opinion that the seasons are a good month or two out of synch with the weather. That when the days really start to stretch out it's only spring and, heat-wise, we're rather lagging behind. Then, before you know it, it's getting on for the longest day and you find yourself thinking, 'Hang on a sec. What the hell are you talking about? *Mid-summer*? There's barely been a week when it's been properly hot.' The seasons just need a bit of a nudge – one way or the other . . . I'm not entirely sure which way – then we could all relax a little and it would all make a lot more sense.

While we're on the subject of vegetables, I once read an article somewhere about a report regarding asparagus and how it makes one's pee smell rather musty. It's one of those odd little things, and I must say I've certainly noticed it myself. In fact, I'm sure most people have. Which is rather the point since, according to this report, the population can be clearly divided into people, like me, whose pee smells powerfully pungent after they've been at the asparagus and those whose pee smells just the same.

Anyway, a couple of months ago I was leafing through the Sunday papers, which of course contain very little news at all and consist mainly of prattle and titbits which have been dressed up as something important, when I tripped over an article which claimed to have the latest news on asparagus and pee-related mustiness, and how some new research suggests that the reason some of us smell it and some of us don't is, in fact, nothing at all to do with what's in the urine, and everything to do with what's going on in the nose. It transpires that only some of us have the olfactory wherewithal to identify the scent. Apparently, every last one of us produces musty-smelling pee after eating asparagus. It's just that not everyone can pick it out. Which rather encourages one to take the latest scientific proclamations regarding diet, etc., with a healthy pinch of salt.

You hear about these couples who retire to the country and how hubby does all the driving – how, in fact, she doesn't drive at all. Then, three or four months into their new rural life, when they've barely started the redecorating, he has a heart attack. And suddenly she's out in the middle of nowhere, doesn't know anyone, and there's only one bus into town every second Wednesday and Country Life doesn't seem like such fun after all.

You can either read it as a cautionary tale against moving out to the sticks when you're in your sixties or becoming too dependent on one's spouse. With regards to the latter, in all fairness, I think it rather creeps up on you. In our house I always tended to take care of the domestic bills, etc. – not necessarily because I'm such a whiz with a spreadsheet, but because I probably just had more time. So I suppose I should just be thankful that I'm not one of those widows who's never seen a gas bill and goes into anaphylactic shock at the very thought of one. It tends to be men who don't have a clue how to operate the cooker, or imagine the creation of spag bol to be a thing of great complexity. But then, given the current standard of my diet, I'm not really in a position to criticise.

It's the solitariness (if such a word even exists) that floored me. You suddenly appreciate how that husband of yours – the one you always moaned about – was such a significant fixture. If only in the sense that his routine (what time he left for work . . . what time he got back, etc.) gave your day some structure around which to organise your own. Otherwise, you really do start to rattle about the place. And the chores really do suddenly seem a complete and utter waste of time. Not that I ever aspired to be the 1950s idea of a housewife with the pinched waist, pointy tits and proud smile as I placed some frazzled carcass on the table (with those little paper chefs' hats covering the ends of the ribs). It's just that you do somehow end up using the person you share your life with as some sort of motivation for getting things done. Even if you do rather resent it at the same time.

For me, the epitome of the desperation of solo living these days is having to drag the wheelie bin out to the road before dawn on a Tuesday morning. Then dragging the bloody thing back in the afternoon. And it's not simply that I want John to be doing it for me. There just seems to be something supremely futile to it. 'How many more bloody times', I would wonder, 'am I going to drag this stupid great lump of plastic up and down the bloody drive?'

And in the evening there's no one to ask if you'd remembered to do it. Or to whom you can say, 'Those damned bin men didn't come round again.' One of the biggest shocks upon joining the ranks of the widowed/ widowered is that Bin News is something you tend to keep to yourself. Unless you happen to collar some unsuspecting neighbour and get it off your chest to them.

Apparently, wheelie bins haven't quite made it up to north Norfolk yet. Either they drag their metal dustbins out into the lane or just pile their bin bags up in a great heap. It's all terribly olde-worlde. Wednesday is bin day. I'd put it in my diary if I had one. Maybe I'll put it on a list.

One or two of the villagers have started nodding at me. We are, officially, on nodding terms. Who knows, another year or two and we might actually have a conversation. I suppose they're used to people pitching up for a week and doing the whole 'Hail fellow, well met' routine on the way to the paper shop, then the next week they're gone, and someone else is unloading the car. And the people who were super-friendly are back home in the city being miserable again.

On the subject of redecorating, I find it very hard as I sit before the fire of an evening not to speculate as to precisely what I'd do with this place if I actually owned it. And not just re which carpets to take up (A: all of them). Or which woodchipped walls to strip (see answer to previous question). But how to rejig the kitchenette in such a way as to create a little more storage space, or even sufficient room to be able to turn around.

You wouldn't want to start knocking down walls, partly because there aren't actually any to knock down except the one between the bedrooms, since one of the few things this cottage has got going for it is its modest dimensions. It sort of fits quite snugly around you. I'm sometimes sitting at this table or slumped in the armchair and it occurs to me that if I reached my arms out I might be able to touch both walls. Of course, I couldn't. But I wouldn't be far off. And the idea that I might be able to reassures me somehow.

There's a terrific film called *The Awful Truth* – a sort of screwball comedy, with a plot not a million miles away from *The Philadelphia Story,* in as much as a woman endeavours to start a new life with a new man, only to be forced in the end to accept that nothing less than Cary Grant will do. Well I'm not about to argue with that. Anyway, there are a couple of scenes that are absolutely priceless, one of which has been rattling round my head all afternoon.

Cary Grant plays . . . well, pretty much the same character he plays in all his pictures. But in this instance the wife from whom he's separated, played by the lovely Irene Dunne, is in the process of hitching her wagon to some Texan millionaire who's made all his money from oil, or something equally vulgar. Anyway, the three of them happen to bump into each other in some Manhattan nightspot and Irene Dunne, despite clearly being far too sophisticated for the oilman, is doing her best to pretend she's having a rare old time. Cary Grant insists they all have a drink together, and at some point the oilman lets slip, much to Irene's embarrassment, that he's managed to talk her into moving to Oklahoma. Well, we see this big, cheesy grin spread across Cary Grant's chops. And he says how that sounds simply *wonderful*, and proceeds to list the many benefits of such a move. Then wraps it up by saying that, of course, if it gets a little dull in Oklahoma City, you can always go over to *Tulsa* for the weekend.

It's the way he sort of coughs out the word 'Tulsa', as if clearing something unpleasant from the back of his throat. That and the evil glint in his eye. Anyway, it makes me hoot every time I see it. I'm just annoyed that I can't think of the name of the actor who plays the oilman, who's extremely funny, and rather cast against type.

Actually, what bothers me more is the fact that I have precisely no idea why that particular scene popped into my mind today and took up such tenacious residence. If I were deluded I might think it was because the set-up – viz. a woman, her husband and her lover – was somehow similar to mine at the time that I was seeing Paul. There's no denying that I've been thinking about that particular little episode an awful lot lately. But the reason I'd have to be mad to make the comparison is because that would somehow involve my recently deceased husband, John, being represented by Cary Grant. Which is about as unlikely as me being played by Irene Dunne.

The closest John and Paul ever came to crossing paths was when Paul came down to London and stayed for a single night. Even as I write that down I can't help but think what an insanely reckless and selfish thing that was for me to do.

John was away from the Friday right through till the Sunday and it seemed that Paul still had the last scraps of appetite for a woman fifteen years his senior who was intent on throwing herself at him. He was down in London for some meeting, but wasn't at all keen on the idea of us being together in my marital home. Which, funnily enough, was quite the opposite of how I felt. I wanted to screw in every room . . . on every stair . . . on every inch of carpet. I wanted to desecrate the place.

Rather frustratingly, once I'd finally managed to get him into the house Paul came over all coy. He wanted to shower without me squeezing in beside him. Then wandered round the rooms, studying the bookshelves and the framed pictures like a visitor to a National Trust property. To such a degree, in fact, that I began to think that him seeing the things I shared with John, far from heightening the illicit thrill of the infidelity, actually fixed in his mind the idea of me and John as a long-standing couple and, who knows, perhaps even induced in him some sympathy for the man whom he was cuckolding.

In fact, I now accept that it made not the slightest difference. The affair, by that point, was practically dead on its feet. Another huff and a puff and the whole thing would come tumbling down.

Paul came creeping in by cover of darkness. We had a bottle of wine, ate some food and watched a movie. But within an hour, I could see that having him round had been a dreadful error. At his insistence we slept in the spare bedroom. Apparently, sleeping in another man's bed crosses some moral threshold which one stops just short of when screwing his wife.

And all through the night, after our most perfunctory

and, as things turned out, final act of fornication, I could sense that he was half-awake – listening out . . . for what exactly? Presumably, John's car pulling into the drive. Such a thing would have entailed all sorts of hopping-about and pulling-on-of-socks and leaping-out-of-windows and other such carry on. Which, again, would have probably delighted me no end. I explained several times that John never came back early, but he wouldn't have it. Until, finally, I just left him to it. If you want to spend the whole night on tenterhooks, I thought, then be my guest.

By seven o'clock the next morning Paul was up, had tossed a cup of coffee down his throat and was out the door. Gee, I thought, this is like having a second husband. Or would have done if I hadn't been so busy flapping and fretting and getting all emotional. And, in spite of everything, still desperately trying to come up with a way of breathing a little life back into my failing affair.

John arrived back about seven or eight on the Sunday evening. As the hours passed I found myself becoming increasingly disappointed. There was no sniffing of the air (another man's sweat . . . another man's presence). And in the days which followed, no unfamiliar strand of hair drawn out of the shower plughole, or other incriminating evidence presented to me. No neighbours stopped John in the street with whispers regarding a certain young man seen tiptoeing into the house last thing at night, or tiptoeing out first thing in the morning. In fact, no sense of impending drama of any sort.

I finally knew that it was over when I rang Paul a couple of days later. I stood in the phone box at the allotted hour and dialled his number but the phone just kept on ringing. I must have known what was coming, but heroically refused to see it, dialling again every couple of minutes until I finally managed to get hold of him. Perhaps I should have just taken it on the chin. Or threatened to kill him, like any normal, well-adjusted gal. Instead, I decided that what was called for was a good deal more supplication and degradation (desperation always being so appealing at such times).

Under duress, he admitted that, as far as he was concerned, the wheels had indeed come off our little adventure. Actually, 'admitted' is some way short of appropriate. He 'announced' it, as if this was the culmination of several hours' rehearsal, distilling his little soliloquy, if I remember rightly, down to no more than three or four bullet points. And, I suspect, telling himself as he did so that in the circumstances it was the most merciful thing to do.

Apparently, the simple facts of the matter were as follows: (i) it had been tremendous fun while it lasted . . . (ii) we were both grown-ups (although I can't quite remember what bearing this had on anything) . . . and that (iii) he now had to get on with his life, without, it naturally followed, me clinging to his trouser legs.

I was informed that I really was a lovely woman – as if it might be something I'd consider adding to my CV when applying for any future extra-marital shenanigans.

But strangely, my current loveliness seemed to have very little in common with the loveliness he'd first divined in me down in Devon – a quality which so possessed him that he had no choice but to proposition me. No, the word 'lovely' in this context was strangely neutered. The kind of word you'd use to describe a biscuit. Or someone else's child.

In fact, it took another couple of phone calls and a great deal of shouting and tears on my part, and stony silences on his, before he finally admitted that there was another factor in the equation. Which was that . . . (iv) the ex-girlfriend (the one whose departure had caused him such heartbreak and provoked such disingenuous sympathy from me) was miraculously back on the scene.

Within a matter of seconds of telling me – it seems to me now it was the very next sentence – he told me that I must *not*, under any circumstances, try to contact him again. And that if I did he would get in touch with John and tell him what we'd been up to. So that, in that instant, I found myself transformed from newly anointed ex-lover to fully fledged hysteric. A danger from which the new woman in his life must be protected at all costs.

I actually did ring again, a week or two later, but the number wasn't registered. He must've changed it. I wonder what complicated excuse he came up with to his ex and now reinstated girlfriend as to why he had to do that?

And, I swear to God, but it's just this second occurred to me . . . why I keep thinking of that little scene from *The*

Awful Truth. My own set-up was indeed a little triangle. But it wasn't Paul and John, with me in the middle. It was Paul and me and Paul's ex. I'm not Irene Dunne. Paul is. I'm the bloody oilman. The one whose name I can't remember. The one who longs to live in Oklahoma and whose eyes roll back in their sockets whenever he breaks into the chorus of 'Home on the Range'.

I'm rather taken with my new binoculars. When you've finished using them they sort of fold up into themselves, and are altogether quite ladylike – in that they're not so big that if you happen to spin around when they're round your neck you're likely to take anyone's eye out. Not that I'm ever in close enough proximity to anyone these days to have to worry about that. Having the chap in the shop hand me three different pairs of binoculars this morning was about as intimate an encounter I've had for quite some time. Close enough, certainly, for me to detect the distinct whiff of cough sweet about him as he talked.

I'd actually prepped myself with the names of a couple of wading birds, which I'd picked out from some identification chart I'd found in a drawer here at Widow's Cottage. But as I stood there among all those quilted waistcoats and Barbour jackets I explained that I was only a budding birdwatcher, so he couldn't have expected me to be especially knowledgeable. And within a couple of minutes we'd narrowed it down to two or three models and I was standing on the shop's doorstep trying to read the road signs at the far end of the street.

I found my focus drifting onto pedestrians – a couple of youths . . . a woman pushing a buggy . . . some old chap standing waiting with his dog. There's something very pleasing (and, of course, entirely reprehensible) about observing people when they're not aware of it. Although, when you're out in the street you always accept that you are, to some degree, on show.

'And you know the first rule of birdwatching?' the salesman asked me.

I brought the binoculars away from my face. I don't believe I did.

'When you spot something interesting, with the naked eye . . .' he said and pointed across the road, as if the year's first yellowhammer had just alighted on the post box, ' . . . you keep right on looking . . .' which he did, with great intensity, like Superman burning a hole through a piece of steel, ' . . . then bring the binoculars up to your face.'

He slowly raised his cupped hands, which held a pair of invisible binoculars.

'Otherwise, you'll lose it,' he said. 'And by the time you've worked out where you were meant to be looking the bloody thing's halfway back to Africa.'

To be honest, this sounds like the kind of hokum only a non-bona-fide birdwatcher would be spouting. Rule number one for proper birdwatchers would, I imagine, be something to do with finding a decent location. Or not wearing scratchy-sounding waterproofs. But you got the idea that he was the kind of chap who if you did anything but agree with him you'd be there all bloody day.

Anyway, I really am very pleased with my purchase. After lunch I took them out for a little spin on the saltmarshes. I stared out towards the horizon. Then east and west along the coast. On my way home I stopped and scanned the low hill between the villages. There are one or two large houses up there in the trees. No one was out and about. If they had been I'm fairly confident that I would have seen them. Would've probably been able to pick out a fellow human being within half a mile of me. And quite right, considering the amount of money they cost me. By my reckoning, the local exchange rate is roughly three pairs of binoculars to one second-hand car.

Physical intimacy, it almost goes without saying, has been all but absent for a little while longer than these first few months of widowhood. Over the last ten years things have been pretty quiet, carnally. There may have been the odd week here and there when we seemed to rediscover the joys of a bit of intercourse, and I'd find myself thinking, 'Actually, this is rather good fun.' But then something would interrupt it, the ennui would creep back in, and the one night when you're in the mood he isn't, and vice versa. Even if, by then, the rejection is partly out of spite for having been refused yourself a few nights before. Until the not having sex becomes the norm again. And, all of a sudden, you can count the months since you last did it, and the years since you did it in anything but the most rudimentary way.

But we always shared a bed. From time to time, after the lights went out, one of us would whisper, 'I love you.' And mean it, despite it sounding so desperate. Especially in the dark, when there was a good couple of feet between us. And hearing those words would do nothing but remind us how our relationship seemed so lacking in anything like real love.

John would fall asleep in a matter of minutes. Once the lights went out there'd be the double-cough, then the long sigh/exhalation. Two minutes later he'd roll over onto his side, so that he was facing away from me. Then he'd be gone.

It's hard not to resent such a capacity. Especially when, within a couple of minutes, his snoring would be contributing to my being awake. Sometimes I'd get up and tiptoe off into the spare room, to read or listen to the radio. And, of course, if I'd wanted I could have stayed up all night, listening to some unabridged Austen or Brontë. Or making endless lists. I could've quite easily kitted out one of the spare rooms properly and moved in there wholesale. But, to be honest, it wouldn't have felt quite right. I've got friends who have perfectly loving relationships with husbands who now sleep in opposite ends of the house, either because of the snoring or the different hours they keep. But with me and John it was always important for us to maintain the conjugal bed, even if there wasn't much conjugation to speak of. It was just where we retreated to at the end of the day. And the fact that our relationship had changed, and possibly even failed, in all sorts of ways was put to one side. We just liked knowing that the other person was there.

I remember going to Rome sometime in the 1970s. It may have been my very first visit. We were only there for a couple of days, before moving on to somewhere else. I don't recall what John was doing – probably drinking Italian beer and reading an English newspaper – but I'd gone wandering off on my own, and came out into one of the big piazzas, and just strolled into a church to have a look around.

It was a beautiful place. And so utterly different from anything I'd seen before, with all this incredible gilding and ornamentation . . . amid a rather grand dilapidation. Anyway, after I'd stood and looked up at the ceiling for a couple of minutes I had a walk around and found this magnificent painting. A huge, great thing it was. And I was still standing there gawping at it when some old lady came along and stood beside me. After a little while she said something to me. Unfortunately, my Italian was close to non-existent. She was pointing and nattering away, and for all I knew was casting some ancient Italian curse on me.

I wasn't exactly thrilled with the situation – didn't have a clue what I'd done to upset her. And the more I tried to explain that I didn't understand her, the more agitated she became. Until, finally, she grabbed my hand and prised apart my fingers. I was thinking, Oh my God, now the crazy old witch is going to read my palm, and tell me what a miserable life I've got stretched out before me. Or how I'm going to get knocked down by a horse before I've even reached my prime.

Then she placed a coin in my hand. And pointed to the wall just below the painting. Well, I was still completely baffled. Still dithering and flapping. But she kept on pointing, until I bent over and saw a metal box on the wall, with a little slot in the top. So I took the coin she'd given me and popped it in, and the moment it clunked inside, the whole wall lit up. It was almost blinding. And the painting that I'd just been squinting at was suddenly bathed in light.

I've forgotten which painting it was now, but there's every chance that it was a Caravaggio. I'd like it to have been a Caravaggio. Some writhing, reaching tangle of limbs and bodies. Full of blood and lust and anger. Or an apostle with dirt on his feet and down his fingernails. One of the ones that landed him in all sorts of hot water. Whatever it was, having the light suddenly come flooding onto it made it feel like a revelation. An illumination, in both senses of the word.

I'm sure that the principal reason for having a coin-operated light above a painting, as I soon discovered they have in churches right across Rome and Italy, is to protect such priceless works of art from unnecessary exposure, as well as generating a little money along the way. But it must have occurred to someone, at some time or other, that the actual mechanics allow the viewer to have their own personal epiphany. And I must say that I, for one, truly appreciated it.

My daily walks have gradually been venturing ever more westward. I would have hiked all the way there and got the bus back if it were practical, but realistically even that's too much of a stretch. So in the end I just used my little car for what little yellow cars are designed for and drove out there. It can't have taken me more than half an hour.

I've dropped by a couple of times already – once soon after I first arrived and again a few days ago. On my most recent visit I parked up in the village and was leaning against the car, pulling my boots on when the front door of the nearest cottage flew open and some irate little man stuck his stupid head out to tell me precisely where I was and wasn't allowed to park.

Apparently, people out in the sticks are of the opinion that not only do they own their own drive and the stretch of road in front of their garden, but the fifty feet of road to left and right. He actually rather startled me, but I just carried on tying my boots. And when he paused to take a breath I assumed an expression of extreme bewilderment and called out to him, 'Hang on. Didn't you park on *my* street the other day?'

This succeeded in tripping the old bugger up for a couple of seconds.

'Which street is that then?' he said.

'Exactly,' I said, and pointed an accusatory finger at him. Then I slammed the car boot, turned and went stomping off up the lane. I believe I may have muttered, '... you bloody moron,' under my breath as I went. In fact, I know I did.

I have to say, I felt pretty pleased with myself – for standing up to him and for coming up with what seemed like quite a sharp little riposte, right off the cuff. Of course, nobody likes being called a moron – not even a moron – and I hadn't gone very far before I began to wonder whether he might've heard me. And if he had, whether I might return to my car to find that he'd been slashing my tyres, etc. Which was a little unlikely, considering it would've been pretty clear who'd done it. And meant I would've just come back a little later and smashed all his windows. Oh, it's easy to see how these things get out of hand.

So, despite the principle, I vowed not to park there next time. And this morning managed to find a little patch of ground at the side of the lane where people had obviously parked before, away from any houses and not blocking any gates to fields, or likely to upset the natives in any conceivable way.

I walked across a couple of fields and joined the coastal path without much trouble. And it was only half a mile or so from there over to the reserve. I've been up and down that path a few times now, half expecting to just bump into him. And earlier this week I found the point where the path is closest to the cottage, which, to be fair, is not that close at all.

Thanks to my expensive new binoculars I have a pretty good shot at seeing what's going on there. I should certainly be able to see if anyone comes or goes. Which, unfortunately, they didn't. I found a nice little spot, not far from where I came and pitched up however many years ago it is now. And, having reminded myself of it, became quite upset and had to sit down for a couple of minutes to try and pull myself together.

Anyway, apart from seeing the cottage and apparently nobody being in it and getting upset all over again I didn't get an awful lot more done today. Although I like to think I got in some practice at pretending to be a budding birder – a performance which consists of little more than staring into space, sometimes through a pair of binoculars. And nodding knowingly at the few authentic birders who happen to cross my path.

If you're not careful, the way the story ends will ruin the memory of whatever went before it. In fact, it has nothing to do with being careful. That's just the way it is. It's human nature, I suppose, to turn everything into a story. And when we look back at a particular incident we can't help but see it through the prism of what's in between.

It's happening with John. Why wouldn't it? Death casts an awfully long shadow. It happened with Paul as well. I now find it pretty much impossible to recall us sitting on Holkham Sands, all wrapped up in each other's arms, without seeing black clouds on the horizon. Sometimes I want to tell that younger version of myself to enjoy every last second. Sometimes I want to warn her how badly it's all going to end.

Two or three weeks after my little affair finally hit the buffers I came up here, booked into the same hotel I'd stayed at earlier and just sort of drifted around Paul's general neighbourhood like some malevolent spirit. Actually, that's not quite true, because, to be fair, I had next to no ill intent. On the contrary. I somehow imagined that Paul would miraculously sense my presence and see the error of his ways.

The words 'glutton' and 'punishment' come to mind, for some reason. And, in retrospect, it's hard not to feel that, rather than beat myself up, a little wrath directed towards the chap in the cottage might have been more appropriate.

I wandered up and down the path and did a little spying, and spent a couple of hours sitting in his local, quite petrified lest he actually walk through the door. Then, when I was pretty sure I'd plumbed the very depths of self-loathing, I got back in my car and drove home.

It would be fair to say that I pretty much went to pieces. I have no idea how long that particular depression lasted, or how I finally managed to coax myself out of it. What I do remember is a little scene with me and John in the kitchen. And me being snippy with him over something or other. Honestly, I hardly knew I was doing it. But he suddenly exploded, and said, 'I've no idea what the hell is eating away at you. But whatever it is I wish you'd get over it. Because I'm heartily sick of you taking it out on me.'

Or something along those lines.

It's not often I will admit to being totally silenced. I'll usually come up with something, even if it's not very nice. But I was still nailed to the spot and standing there, open-mouthed, when John turned and marched off to another part of the house. I really don't think it had occurred to me that I was being so horrible to him. I mean, I knew that I was feeling bad – about as bad as I'd ever felt. And when you feel bad it's only natural to want to spread it around. But even I could see that if there was one person who didn't deserve to get it in the neck for the failure of my affair it was the man to whom I'd been unfaithful. The sudden appreciation of which did nothing but make me loathe myself even more.

I was in the pub the other night at my usual table and, I imagine, two or three drinks to the good because I'm not usually one to strike up a conversation with complete strangers. But I'd noticed that the couple on the next table had an OS map spread out before them and were trying to come up with some way to occupy themselves the following day. It sounded as if they just wanted to go for a walk and were starting to get a little fractious, since they weren't really familiar with the area. So, like some slightly inebriated fairy godmother, I leant over and suggested one or two walks they could do.

They were there again the following evening and told me how they'd followed my advice and what a wonderful day they'd had, and so on. And I found myself being hailed as the fount of all things local, despite the fact that I only pitched up here myself a couple of weeks ago. The woman, who was a few years younger than me, asked if I lived in the village. And before I knew it I heard myself confiding to her that I'd actually grown up in the area and how I was now spending a month or two in a rented cottage while I contemplated moving back here permanently.

It wasn't so much the lie – or even the lie's dimensions – which shook me, so much as the utterly shameless way in which it came galloping out of me. One could argue that the latter half of the yarn might actually hold some water – though even the idea of me scouting the area for somewhere to live was fairly pushing it. It was the notion of my having spent several years of some apple-cheeked childhood in north Norfolk, wandering around the local meadows – if such a thing exists in this part of East Anglia – making daisy chains with my non-existent sisters, and all of us dressed in matching pinafores.

Then I was on my way back from the shop yesterday when the same couple crossed the road to join me. They seemed to be going in my general direction. And the chap – Donald, I believe he's called – said that they'd been wondering if I'd care to come round to their cottage for dinner. Nothing fancy. Just a bit of pasta, or maybe a nice piece of fish. And, again, as if suddenly possessed, I heard myself apologise, but explain that unfortunately I'd already arranged to meet a friend in a nearby village, but thanks for asking. Then I headed straight into Widow's Cottage, and watched in horror as they carried on down the alley and went into a cottage about four doors away.

What on earth is the matter with me? Is there some medication I've neglected to take? Not that long ago I was quite desperate for company. But now, when someone actually invites me round for dinner what do I do but turn and run. To be honest, I wonder if there isn't some sort of snobbery at work here – that, in a nutshell, I simply have no desire to fraternise with anyone who's been up here even less time than me. Or perhaps I was so embarrassed by my earlier flights of fancy that I daren't spend more than a couple of minutes in their company in case I'm caught out. Or have to sit there and witness even taller tales pour out of me.

On the other hand, it might just be that I genuinely don't want to be spending the whole evening with a couple of near-strangers, no matter how kind and considerate they appear to be. Perhaps I'm doing us both a favour? By the time they opened the second bottle of Pinot Grigio they'd be thinking, Christ on a bike, this woman's completely nuts.

Anyway, in an act of self-flagellation I must've rerun our little conversation in my head a hundred times. But it wasn't until an hour or so later that it occurred to me that, having announced that I had plans for that evening, it would now look pretty peculiar if I just sat in the cottage on my own all night. And I couldn't very well hide out in the pub – either pub, come to that – in case they happened to pop in there and trip right over me. So, short of turning all the lights out and just lying on the living-room floor in the dark for the entire evening, I decided to drive out to a pub in one of the villages, where I spent a weirdly sober couple of hours sipping tomato juice (with a dash of Worcestershire sauce, for extra pep) and reading the paper from front to back.

By half past nine I'd had enough and went out to the car, already fretting about how I was going to have to creep back down the alley to the cottage. But between closing the car door and starting the engine my plans apparently changed and I found myself pulling out of the car park and, instead of heading east back towards the cottage, headed west along the coast.

I left the car at my usual spot, and carried on along the road for ten or fifteen minutes until I reached the point at which the little lane turns off it and leads up towards the reserve. Of course, I didn't have a torch, so as soon as I was under the trees I was bumbling about all over the place. But my eyes slowly got used to the dark, and after fifty yards or so I could see the house lights in the distance and just followed the lane towards them.

The cottage has its own tiny drive, so I tiptoed between the gateposts into it. Then I just stood there, looking. Wanted to be certain it was the right place. There were no other houses anywhere near it. But when I could finally make out the little lean-to at one end that confirmed it for me.

The lights were on in the hallway, but there was no way of knowing whether anyone was home or not. It looked like a lovely little place – felt lived-in and small enough to be cosy. I was edging my way across the lawn when I caught my foot against something and nearly fell right over. I just about managed to keep my balance and bent down, to see what'd nearly tripped me. It was a child's bicycle, lying on its side in the grass, where it'd been abandoned. Judging by its size and the fact that it wasn't fitted with stabilisers I estimated that it belonged to a boy of about five or six years old.

I was still bent over, staring at the bike, when the tops of the trees to my left were suddenly splashed with white light, and I heard the crunch of gravel as a car began to make its way along the lane.

I hadn't a clue what to do. And for a few seconds I just crouched there, stock-still, as the car slowly bobbed in out of the potholes and headed towards me. I thought about running round the back of the cottage but doubted I had enough time to do so. Thought about heading off into the trees, but had no idea what was out there, and was pretty sure there was some sort of fence in the way. So by the time I'd finally managed to snap myself out of my little trance my only option was to run back across the lawn towards the gateposts, with every chance of tripping over another bike along the way, but managed to stay upright until I reached the edge of the garden, then ducked down, just as the car went by.

I didn't move. Then I worked out that the car had actually carried on up the track, and had no intention of turning into the garden. It must have been heading off towards the visitor centre or some other building up there.

I couldn't have cared less. I just counted my blessings, got to my feet and went stumbling back down the lane as quick as was humanly possible. And before the people in the car had finished doing whatever it was they were doing and came along after me.

I just want to see him. To know that he's still alive. I really do believe that will provide me with some solace. To know that there's someone close at hand who once cared for me – possibly even loved me. For me to explain it more coherently I'd have to understand it better myself. But it's as if knowing that he's there would give me something to cling onto. And give me sufficient reassurance to go limping on for another week or two.

Throughout this whole dreadful episode that has been the biggest nightmare. The sense sometimes that it's simply not going to be possible to navigate my way through the next few moments, let alone the weeks and months beyond. I think back to how I felt when I was in my late teens and early twenties. I may not have been deliriously happy, but things at least seemed possible. There was space for me to move into. Whereas, these days, there are moments when I seem to have run right out of options and I can't think how on earth I'll carry on.

I've reached a couple of conclusions lately. Firstly, that trying to watch the house from the path is almost completely impractical – due to the trees, which tend to obscure things, but also the actual distance involved. They are indeed back, from their holidays or wherever they've been. The next time I was out there I could just about make out their car parked up in the garden. And could see various lights on in the house. But not much else. So I checked up and down the path to make sure no one was approaching, then slipped down the bank and climbed over the fence.

The ground beneath the trees is incredibly boggy – more like a swamp than woodland – and within twenty yards the water had come right over the tops of my boots. But I carried on, and kept my head down. And about halfway between the path and the cottage I reached a tumble-down wall, covered in moss, where I sat, all huddled up, for a while. Then brought up my binoculars. And from there I had a much better view of what was going on.

There wasn't a great deal of activity. In fact, there was precisely none. I must have sat there, against my mossy old wall, for well over an hour, with my feet soaking in ice-cold water and my backside slowly going numb. But nobody came or went. And this led quite quickly to my second conclusion, which is that I'm probably watching the cottage at the wrong time of the day.

So I went back to the shop where I bought my binoculars and bought their greenest waterproof jacket – indeed, I would've bought a proper military-style, camouflaged jacket if they'd stocked them. And last night, before bed, I made myself a sandwich and a flask of coffee, and by half past five this morning I was up and driving down the coast road in the pitch dark. Then making my way out to the coastal path. And slipping down that bank towards the trees before there was even a hint of light in the sky.

I had my little torch with me, but there's not much point wearing a jacket that you hope is going to help you blend into the landscape then letting everyone know your whereabouts by flashing a torch all over the place. So I held one hand over the glass, to try and minimise it. And just turned it on for a second at a time, to give me some rough idea where I was.

It was about quarter to seven when the first light went on in the cottage. I wasn't actually watching. I must have been looking somewhere else. But when I looked back I could tell straight away that something was different. And when I had a peep through the binoculars I could pick it out, in one of the upstairs windows. I imagine it was someone going to the bathroom. Then, a couple of minutes later, a second light went on downstairs.

For the next half an hour or so, nothing much happened. Just various lights, and some movement around them. And, let me tell you, half an hour out in the woods in the middle of winter can seem like a very long time.

I had a pretty good view of the little porch at the front of the cottage. Or, rather, I was looking at it from quite a good angle, despite the cottage still being some way away. So when the woman emerged I could see her quite clearly. I couldn't make out her features. She was just a woman, in a coat and hat, getting into a car. But, of course, assuming she was who I thought she was, she was a good deal more than that.

She reversed out onto the lane and once she'd driven off

it was back to the stillness. For another good half an hour or so at least. I could've had a cup of coffee, or eaten my sandwich. But I was convinced that the very next second Paul would come walking out. So I just squatted there with my elbows resting on that old, damp wall, staring through my binoculars, with my heart beating ten to the dozen. Until, finally, I saw the lights go out in the cottage and Paul appeared.

He had two young children with him. One barely toddling. The other – presumably, the one whose bike I tripped over – pottering about the place with a fair amount of confidence. There was a general herding of children towards the second car. A back door was opened and each child was strapped into their seat. When the doors were closed Paul went round to the driver's side. He was about to get in when he paused and looked around, just for a second. I don't honestly think he was looking in my direction or contemplating anything to do with me. He might have just been wondering if he'd remembered to turn the heating off. Or checking that he had his wallet with him. He was a fair distance away, and, like his wife, all wrapped up against the cold. But as he stood there, for those precious few seconds, I watched him with such intensity it was as if I fixed him in my mind. I held him there. And ever since, I keep referring back to that moment. Him standing by the car. And I keep thinking, 'There he is. There he is again.'

Things seem to have fallen into some sort of pattern. For the first time in many months I'm close to having a routine again. Plus I'm beginning to eat a little better. Or, at the very least, more regularly. I somehow seem to have drummed up a bit of an appetite.

There's the odd moment when I consider what I'm doing and worry that I've gone completely loco. That I'm on the verge of doing something dreadful, etc. But then I fill my flask and stuff a couple of tuna rolls into my pocket and go merrily on my way.

I've thought about coughing up the five or ten pounds and trooping round the actual reserve with all the regular punters. I suspect that, with a little forethought, I could quite easily contrive to trip over him. But I'd like our encounter, when it finally happens, to be a bit more intimate. I don't want anyone else wandering in and spoiling the scene.

I did something rather reckless this lunchtime. I'd slept in, and missed them leaving. But I felt the need for a little fix, so I crept through the woods and up to my tumble-down bunker. Then, having checked that both cars had gone I took a deep breath, climbed over the wall and carried on right up to the house.

I had a little walk around it. Peered in through the various windows. This is where they sit to eat their breakfast . . . this is where they sit and watch TV . . . etc.

I sat in the little porch for a couple of minutes. On the opposite side, under the bench, was a load of logs, all neatly chopped and stacked. And on my side, right by my feet were a row of dirty boots and wellingtons, big and small.

It's a lovely little porch. The actual front door is a solid old thing, probably the same age as the house and painted a beautiful deep green. I sat and looked at it for a minute. Some of the paint was worn away below one of the keyholes, presumably where the other keys on the ring have rattled against it over the years. So you could see the bare wood revealed beneath it, and all the layers of paint in between. The paint on the rest of the door was pretty much pristine. Had an almost perfect finish, like plastic. And I had this peculiar urge to puncture that perfect finish. To carve my name, or maybe just my initials into it somewhere. In a corner. Just to say, I'm still here. I haven't gone away.

If I could've found a bit of wood sharp enough to do some decent scratching I would've done so, but I couldn't. All I really need, I thought, is a little vegetable knife. And I made a mental note to try and remember to bring one along next time around.

Going right up to the house really was pretty stupid. Paul could've quite easily popped back at any moment – just to pick something up. Of course, that in itself wouldn't necessarily have been the end of the world. Except that when we meet I very much want to be in control of the situation. For once I would like to decide how things unfold.

My mobile phone is as dead as a dodo. The battery packed up about two weeks ago. Which is no major privation, but may well have made life a little easier today, in that the bank might've got in touch to warn me that I'd exceeded the limit of my overdraft. As it was I had to suffer the indignity of having my card rejected – or should I say, *declined* – at the local shop. Lesser mortals, no doubt, have run outside and doused themselves in petrol following such public humiliation. Personally, it'll take a lot more than the faux embarrassment of some overweight shop assistant to worry me.

But the little to-do in the Spar shop was followed soon after by a dressing-down in the bank in Sheringham, where a youth in a drip-dry shirt took it upon himself to lecture me on the finer points of cash-flow and money-management. I was tempted to say, Have you any idea how much my house is worth, you little dickhead? That big, empty house on top of the hill in north London. The one where I can't watch the telly without flipping my lid. Or how much I have in my savings now that my hubby's popped his clogs. Cut a girl some slack. All I need is enough money to keep myself in booze and fags and tuna sandwiches while I stalk my ex-lover for another couple of days.

But apparently I must seek absolution and overdraft extension from some faceless sage up at head office. Which I flat-out refused to do. So I just withdrew a couple of hundred quid on one of my credit cards and sashayed out of there. Which is the kind of wanton, reckless behaviour that would've brought poor old John out in a nasty rash.

I very nearly buggered things up this morning. I'd been
watching the cottage – to try and get a firm idea of their
routine. They'd gone off to work and I decided to head
back home. And was just scuttling up out of the woods
onto the bank when a proper, fully paid-up birder came
bearing down on me.

I could tell straight away that some sort of explanation
was called for. He looked quite affronted. Presumably
at seeing some woman my age on her hands and knees,
scrambling about the place.

'You know, you shouldn't really be wandering around
in there,' he said. 'That's private property.'

Honestly. What is it with men and territory? I mean,
is it the only way they're able to relate to the world? By
parcelling it up into what's theirs and what isn't, then
getting tetchy at the first hint of an encroachment. Even
when it's on someone else's behalf.

I think the fact that he felt at liberty to be so utterly
patronising to a complete stranger rather spurred me on –
in that it put my nose out to such a degree that I switched
immediately from apologetic/pathetic to something far
more combative.

'I needed a pee,' I said. Or declared, perhaps. It was that
other version of myself speaking again now. And I told

him, quite plainly, that I thought I'd been doing everyone a favour by seeking out a little privacy. But that from now on I would simply squat down and pee in the middle of the path for all the world to see.

I'm not sure. Perhaps I'd been a little too graphic. From his expression, you'd think it was just about the most disgusting thing he'd ever heard.

Well, he flustered and blustered about for a couple of seconds. Then he went storming off down the path – his mind quite likely addled for the rest of the day with the image of me defiantly squatting and peeing before him. And I went off in the other direction.

I think I must have been feeling slightly guilty, because five minutes later I came across another pair of birders and went out of my way to stop and have a chat with them.

I asked if they'd seen anything interesting, and they mentioned – with, I suspect, a large helping of false modesty – several birds whose names meant nothing to me. All the same, I had the distinct feeling that I was meant to be impressed. And when they asked if I'd had any luck myself I found I simply couldn't help myself and, perhaps imagining that saying anything with sufficient authority might somehow compensate for my having nothing remotely intelligent to say, I plucked a couple of birds' names out of thin air and pointed down the path to where I'd recently seen them.

The birders both stood and stared right back at me. As if I were drunk. Or deranged. I can't even remember what birds I claimed to have spotted. But I think there's a good chance they were specimens which are currently meant to be nesting in the Arctic. Or South America. Or possibly completely new birds that I'd just invented, by combining bits of other birds' names.

I don't mind the cold and wet. Some days I quite like it. The discomfort. As if I'm punishing myself. I lean against that old wet wall in the semi-darkness and think perhaps today instead of getting light it might just get dark again. And the darkness will wrap its velvet arms around me and the dark wet wood will just swallow me up.

I've really got to get my act together. I'm just going to have to take a breath and actually get on with it. Because if I don't I'm going to be stuck here forever, in my own home-made purgatory. I'll try and do it tomorrow. Maybe I should have a little slug of rum or brandy. Like they used to give the lads in the First World War – to give them courage before sending them up the ladders and over the top.

I've gone too far. This time I've really done it.

I need help. I'm not fucking kidding. I need someone to save me from myself.

I got there early. So early that, having crept off the path, through the trees and up to my wall I realised that I still had quite a while to wait. And, after five or ten minutes, how incredibly tired I was. I thought maybe I'd have a cup of coffee. Then promptly fell asleep.

When I woke, Paul's wife was fiddling in the back of the car, strapping the children into their seats. At least, that's what I assumed she was doing.

So I got myself ready. Paul tends to leave about half an hour later. So after another ten or fifteen minutes I slipped over the wall and crept forward. Right down to the edge of the trees.

God knows how long I waited. It's not important. What's important is that I was now close enough to the cottage that when the front door opened I could hear it from where I was hiding. I felt excited. That's an understatement. I felt as if I was going to pass out. And as soon as I heard the latch I got to my feet and headed up onto the lawn and across the garden. I wanted to intercept him before he reached the car.

What threw me was the fact that he had the children

with him. The little girl in his arms, and the little boy walking. I really hadn't expected that at all. What was the wife doing if not fastening the children into their seats? Who knows. That's history now. The little boy was the first one I encountered. He just sort of froze and looked up at me. And I think it was probably his reaction which caused Paul to stop.

Christ, but I wanted so much for it just to have been the two of us. But what was I going to do but carry on.

'Paul,' I said. 'I need to talk to you . . .'

That's all I wanted. To tell him about John's death. And how utterly miserable I've been. I think I also wanted to tell him how much our little affair had meant to me, but that I am beginning to think that it completely screwed up what was left of my love for my husband. And is now stopping me coming to terms with his death.

I suppose that's quite a lot, but I could've said it quickly. And then been on my way. But he looked so utterly stumped. And so thoroughly worried. As if I might grab his precious children or attempt some other crazy stunt.

Then, as I looked at him, the strangest thing happened. His expression . . . in fact, his whole face began to change. His features altered and he was slowly transformed – from the Paul I knew was meant to be there into someone quite different. And altogether wrong.

He carried on staring at me for another few seconds. And I felt the world begin to flex and bend again.

'Are you sure you've got the right man?' he said.

And now the children were beginning to get upset. The

232

little girl in his arms had started crying. The little boy retreated behind his father's legs. But it wasn't the kids I was worried about. It was me. And it didn't help that the man before me looked so concerned. For my general welfare. Then he was telling me that Paul – the man who used to live here – had moved to France, a good six or seven years ago.

I looked the man full in the face now. He looked nothing like him. It must have been the hat and scarves. That and the fact that I wanted it to be him.

I would rather be dead, I thought. I would rather be dead and buried than standing here like this. Really. What is the fucking point?

I have no idea how I removed myself from the situation. I just found myself running down the lane. Which was, at least, probably more advisable than heading back into the swampy woods.

But when I reached the main road I couldn't quite remember where the car was, or how to get there. I started screaming. And very nearly got myself knocked down as I went careering down the road.

Then, finally, I was back at the car. And sitting in it, with the doors locked. Crying. Crying for God knows how long. Then starting the car, in case he called the police. And just wanting to be away from there. Wanting to be gone.

I've had enough. The relentless struggle just to keep one's head above water. You think, 'I'll just try and get through the morning. And if by then things haven't improved it'll at least be lunchtime.' Because a little food can sometimes change how you feel. And you find yourself opening a tin of tomato soup, thinking, 'I wonder if this is going to stop me cracking up?'

But the cupboard's bare. There's no will. The will's unwilling. And you begin to think, Well, fuck it. That really is quite enough.

It's like hearing two voices, constantly bickering. One pointing out every conceivable misery. The other desperately trying to reason, to negotiate. Which is pretty awful to begin with. But, I swear, the voice of reason has just about jacked it in. It's finding it hard to put up any resistance. It's on the verge of just saying, 'You know what, I think you're probably right.'

When I think about it now I do wonder what the hell I was thinking, prowling round his house like a bloody nutcase. I could've been arrested. Or sectioned. It wouldn't be so bad, but I wasn't even stalking the right bloody man.

In fact, I know very well what I was doing. I just wanted

to get a little nearer to the heat and light of a real home – a place with real love and warmth in it. Like some stray dog, trying to get a little respite from the dark.

I haven't left the village for a good couple of days now. Have hardly set foot out of the cottage. It's been too wet. But the sun could've been blazing down and I still wouldn't have ventured out there. I'd be too embarrassed. I'd feel the entire world was mocking me.

I've begun to miss my house. Which you'd think might be a good thing. What with me owning it and all. But I suspect it's just the idea of home I miss – and that I've been away long enough to have forgotten that John no longer lives there. Well, there's another little myth I've created for myself. The happy home. The loving husband. The imagination of the common or garden melancholic really is something to behold.

Not that long after I first arrived at the cottage I found a leaflet in one of the folders for a circular walk out to a lost village, a few miles south of here.

Perhaps we're just born romantic – or dreamers – but a Lost Village puts me in mind of something hidden. Something waiting to spring back into existence. Or some thriving little fairy-tale community, which somehow slipped between the folds in the landscape and carried on regardless. And maybe that's what I was secretly hoping for when I set off on the walk. A sort of East Anglian Shangri-La.

At the very least, I was expecting a couple of ruined cottages. A chimney stack deep in the woods and one or two walls, all choked in ivy. But when I reached the spot where the map claimed the lost village was located all that was visible were a few low mounds in an open field. If you looked hard enough you could make out where there might once have been lanes. Or drains. Or something. But the whole place had essentially been wiped off the face of the earth. The land had healed right over it. And I'm not exaggerating in the least when I say that it scared me half to death.

About a week after John died I started having problems with time. Serious problems. Problems of such magnitude that I began to question the conventional perception of its passing – namely, a steady unfolding of events along a ruler's edge. Time, or my appreciation of it, fragmented. It seemed to come apart in my hands. There would suddenly be bits missing. It lost its linearity. So that not only would I fail to remember how I got back from the shops that morning, but rather worryingly the memory of my getting home would feel as if it had occurred prior to my going out.

It was a sort of temporal dislocation. Which is a terribly clinical way of describing it, and much too neat and tidy. Because the reality is utterly terrifying in its abstraction. As if one's grip on life has slipped – keeps constantly slipping. As if all the things which are meant to be solid – the very ground on which you walk – are suddenly untrustworthy, and prone to collapse.

What I've endured these last few days is actually quite different. Rather than a sense of fracture or slippage, time has simply stopped. It's not that the clock is malfunctioning. It's that the bloody thing's broke. Moments fail to unfold. And all I'm left with is a dreadful stasis, with just me in it. Nothing but me and my terrifying thoughts.

* * *

I suddenly feel dreadfully vulnerable. Exposed to everything, particularly John's death, which has somehow hit me again these last few days like a juggernaut. Which is rather curious, because what have the last three or four miserable months consisted of, if not the reality of my husband's death making itself known to me in a million different ways?

All I know is that it's a different appreciation. As if I'd managed to run away up here, and perhaps even briefly escape it. Or at the very least put some distance between me and all the pain. Then one morning I looked out of the window to find a removal van pulling up. Packed to the roof with all my emotional baggage and general fucked-upness. And a minute later some bloke is standing on the doorstep, saying, 'Where would you like us to put it, love?'

The old food-to-booze ratio has gone a little pear-shaped. The balance keeps tipping towards the gin. Which would be all very well if it wasn't for the mornings after. Or, rather, the middles of the night, when I suddenly wake, with a small piece of coal burning in the pit of my stomach and another burning in my soul.

I'm slowly pickling myself. I'm going to be a biological phenomenon. Perfectly preserved, in all my widow's glory. They're going to put me in a big glass jar in some dusty museum. The accompanying notice will say, 'Due to all the booze sloshing around in her system this woman managed to live to be 250 years old. Unfortunately, the last couple of hundred were a complete and utter blur.'

I've been at it again. The freaking out . . . the jumping in the car . . . and the driving, pell-mell, through the bloody dark. And, just like the last time, I'd be hard pressed to put my finger on what actually triggered it. It may just be accumulated angst or grief or anger. All of which I have in abundance. Most days I'm like a pan rattling away on the cooker, somewhere between simmering and boiling. Then, every once in a while, suddenly it's – KAPOW. And I'm up and out and at 'em. And driving like a maniac through the night.

I'd had a relatively booze-free evening. I've been so dreadfully tired and I was just desperate for a good night's sleep. But when I finally managed to coax myself up to bed and turned the light out I just lay there, staring at the ceiling. And, within an hour or so, was wishing I'd had a decent dose of alcohol, just to knock me out.

I was feeling particularly sorry for myself. In fact, I was feeling sorry for pretty much the whole of humanity. I don't recall the details, but I do remember becoming increasingly sick and frightened. Had somehow managed to tie myself in knots. Then I started to panic. And felt that if I didn't do something drastic pretty quickly, that I would go mad and stay mad for all eternity.

Quite suddenly, I couldn't lie there any longer. I jumped

out of bed, pulled on some clothes and went clattering down the tiny stairwell. Grabbed my keys and coat. So that in the space of about two minutes I'd gone from lying in bed to striding through the village towards the car.

I headed west along the coast road, with no clear destination in mind. And it was only as I entered Holkham village that I thought of the beach, and it occurred to me that I might actually find myself out there on it. Then I was pulling up beside the gate to the car park. Was climbing over the gate and heading towards the trees.

It felt quite strange, walking along that wide avenue where all the cars are usually parked and for it to be so empty. It seems as if that was the first time I became fully aware of being out in the middle of the night.

I walked right to the end, and instead of creeping round to the left and through the trees, I carried straight on, up the path over the dunes. I could feel my shoes sink into the sand and how heavy it made each step.

At the top of the dunes there was enough light for me to see the beach spread out below me. That infinite beach. I stopped, but for no more than a couple of seconds. Then I carried on down the other side. And, without ever making a conscious decision, I set out across the sands, towards the sea.

It wasn't as if, now that I was walking, I was suddenly relaxed or relieved or deliriously happy. I wasn't. It was just that I was walking, and had a little mission. And that seemed to have taken precedence over whatever was going on in my head.

The sand was firm now, and I could hear the sea way off in the distance, booming and roaring. A quite incredible sound. Halfway there, I remember stopping and taking my shoes and socks off, so that I could actually feel the sand, cold and damp beneath my feet. And, another ten or fifteen minutes later, I could feel how the sand had formed into ripples. Could feel the balls of my feet catch them as I walked. And the booming of the waves was an almighty noise now, and you could smell the salt and dampness in the air.

Then suddenly I was at the water's very edge and cold, cold water was under my feet and rushing round my ankles. Thirty or forty yards out the waves came crashing down and the foam came in, spreading over the flattened water. Came sweeping in all around me.

I still don't know what I was after. I was all tangled up inside myself. In fact, I think I started to pick over the things I'd been worrying about back at the cottage. Started to rake over the embers of my anxieties. And was doing a pretty good job of breathing some life back into them – when something happened. As I stood there, watching those huge waves rolling and crashing, at the very end of my tether. Just when I felt that I'd had quite, quite enough. It was as if . . . as if an undeniable truth briefly revealed itself to me. Which sounds preposterous, I know. But I can't think of another way of putting it. It was as if I had the briefest glimpse of some universal force at work. Of incredible power and infinite grace, which obliterated any thought or worry I might ever have. I might almost say that, in that instant, I finally found myself obliterated – or removed. Which was not the least bit terrifying. And for that briefest, briefest moment I sensed that there might be some grand concordance. That, in fact, contrary to everything I've come to believe in, that the world might be good and kind. And that there might be a place for me in it.

This morning, in the cold light of day, I could rationalise the whole strange experience by saying that, standing before the waves and beneath the stars, I'd simply been overwhelmed or reassured by the force of nature. Or that when one is panicking there comes a point when one's mind and body have simply had enough, and the panic suddenly runs out of steam. Some chemical is released into the bloodstream. So that, after all the chaos and the crashing, there's a sudden release and a spreading smoothness, like the foam on the flat, flat water. And that it's nothing but physiology.

But that's not it. That momentary thought, or revelation, was as real and tangible as anything I've ever encountered. It really was. It was over in a fraction of a second. There were no tears. No angelic chorus. I was the same person I was before. It was just that I'd had this glimpse of something. Then I was back there, with my feet in the water, clutching my shoes, and wondering what on earth had just gone on.

I'm considering buying a map of Britain, and marking on it all the places that have significance for me. Where I first fell in love . . . the artist's studio where I used to be a life model . . . the chapel at the American Cemetery . . . and so on. My own personal stations. I could put a few weeks aside and walk around them, barefoot – to honour them.

I remember standing in the civic square of some English city when I was ten or eleven, in front of a street map in a big glass case. Along the bottom there was a row of buttons. And when you pressed one of the buttons a series of little bulbs lit up across the map, to tell you where the churches were. Another button would illuminate the theatres . . . the libraries and museums . . . etc. All these different little constellations. These necklaces of light.

I fully accept that the stations in my life will mean virtually nothing to the next person. But that doesn't demean them one bit. And when I bring to mind what really gives me pleasure: my walks out across the marshes, for instance, or what brings me joy, like Holbein's Christina of Denmark, then I can say with absolute conviction that these things improve me. Heal me, even. And, when combined, that their power multiplies. Those days I spent on retreat when I was in my twenties . . . the memory of me hanging out the grass to dry . . . even those old ships scratched on the backs of the pews, not far from here.

I'm not quite right yet. I understand that. I suspect I'll never be quite right again. But I also know that if I keep on focusing on all the horrors then I'll do nothing but dig myself an early grave.

It may well be that there is indeed some terrible entropy at work. That everything that is, and ever was, is slowly torn apart. But human beings aren't built for living under those sort of conditions. We need to draw things together. We need to decide what is precious to us. What is sacred. And hold onto them.

Apparently, I just pull the door to and drop the keys through the letter box. The agency has a spare set and will let themselves in.

I've been told that there's a charge for leaving the place unhoovered. But I'll happily pay it. I'm not about to get down on my hands and knees and mop the floor, or clean the fridge out. I haven't got the strength.

I've decided not to mention the severed TV cable. I'm sure when someone notices it they'll get in touch. My only other concern is that I now have two cars in the car park and tend not to drive more than one at a time. I was tempted to ring up dear old Ginny and ask her if she fancied jumping on a train and driving one of them back for me. We could head back to town in our own little convoy. But I'd much rather just turn up on her doorstep and surprise her. I'll decide which one to drive back when I see them. And maybe come and get the other one later on.

Of course, I could just leave the other one up here full-time, and have it as my north Norfolk runabout. For when I visit. I might yet buy myself a little shack. Who knows. Like pretty much everything else these days it's still too early to say.

I shall just get through this week. Then the next one. And see how things look from there.